Th

Adventure Island

The Mystery Series
Book 2

The Mystery of Adventure Island

PAUL MOXHAM

Copyright

CONTENTS

CHAPTER 1

A NEW ADVENTURE

After gazing through the binoculars for several minutes, twelve-year-old Joe Mitchell turned to his two sisters who were sitting beside him on the cliff. "We should ask Will if he knows anyone who can take us there. It looks like a great camping spot."

Amy, the eldest of the two girls, swept back her long, brown hair. "But what would we do if we went there?"

Joe looked back at Lighthouse Island, which was situated just off the coast. Apart from a lighthouse, there was nothing on it except a few bushes and trees. "I know it might not look too exciting, but I bet there are tons of different seabirds there." He glanced at Sarah, the youngest of the three siblings. "What do you think?"

"I think it would be fun," Sarah said, her green eyes shining. "It may not be as much fun as exploring the tunnels underneath Chandler Manor or Bracknesh Castle—"

"I didn't think you liked those places," Amy interrupted. "Last week, after we solved the mystery of the missing gnomes, you said—"

"I know what I said, but that was then and this is now," Sarah interrupted.

Joe smiled. "You know, I never thought that Smugglers Cove could be so much fun, especially since it's smaller than Danfield. I like living close to London, but we seem to be having more adventures here than we ever had at home."

"I wish we could stay forever," Amy said. "But in just over two weeks, we'll be back at St. Mary's." She stood up. "Let's go and talk to Will about going camping."

Climbing onto their bicycles, the children pedalled along the cliff path. They were soon in the main street of the small seaside village of Smugglers Cove. Waving as they passed Constable Biggens, they rode past the shops and houses, stopping when they arrived at a medium sized house.

Joe saw that their red haired friend was in the front garden cleaning his bicycle. "Hello, Will!"

Will glanced up and gave a cheery smile. "Hi."

"Do you know of any good places to go camping?" Amy asked.

Will grinned. "Getting bored, are we?"

"How did you guess?" Joe questioned.

"Well, when I first came here from London just after the war ended, I was bored at first," Will replied. "Of course, you can't say it's been too dull for you. You've had three adventures in four weeks."

"I know," Joe said. "I guess we're just lucky. Anyway, I was wondering about Lighthouse Island. Do you know if there are many birds there?"

Will thought. "I don't think there are, but I haven't been there. The lighthouse was closed a number of years ago, so there hasn't been a reason for anyone to go there. Why?"

"I want to see some birds, and it would be fun camping by ourselves," Joe replied.

"We would need a boat," Sarah piped up.

"Well, we'd only need a rowing boat to go to Lighthouse Island, so I'm sure I could find someone to loan us one." Will dipped his rag into a bucket of water and gave his bicycle a rub. "I have some errands to run, so why don't we meet at the beach in three hours and discuss it then?"

"Sounds good," Joe replied.

~

The afternoon sun shone down on the three children as they raced down the well-worn path that led to the sandy beach. After splashing in the shallow water, they decided to make a sandcastle. They didn't have any buckets to help them move the sand, but they still managed to make a pretty decent castle.

As they waited for the tide to come in, Sarah spotted Will standing up on the cliff path.

Will waved. "Come up here!"

"I wonder why he wants us up there," Amy said.

"Well, there's only one way to find out." Joe raced across the sand with the girls in hot pursuit. Soon, the three had joined Will on the cliff top.

"What's up?" Amy asked.

"Follow me. I've got something to show you." Will turned and walked away.

"What?" Joe asked, curious.

"You'll see," Will replied.

Joe and the girls followed their friend through the streets of Smugglers Cove. As they arrived at the small harbour, Will headed towards an old shed. He put his hand on the door handle. "I talked to my father and…" He paused and flung open the door.

Inside the shed was an assortment of tools and scrap metal and other useless junk, but it was what was in the middle that attracted everyone's attention.

It was a sailboat. Joe's eyes lit up. A real sailboat. Sure, it didn't look like much, but as long as it could float, that was all that mattered. He touched it. "Is this for us to use?"

Will nodded. "My father talked to Quigley, an old fisherman who owns this boat, and he told me that if we wanted to spend some time fixing it up, we could take it out whenever we wanted."

"Does it float?" Sarah asked.

"Well, I can't see any holes in it, so it should." Will walked over and joined the others as they admired the craft. "I know it's pretty old, but it's a boat."

Amy touched the wood and realised it was coated with a thin layer of dust. "Golly! This hasn't been used for ages."

"As long as it can take us to Lighthouse Island, that's all that matters." Joe turned around as a man suddenly entered the shed.

Will smiled. "Hello, Quigley. It's a fine boat."

With deep creases in his brown, weathered face and a white beard, Joe thought the fisherman looked very old. With the aid of a walking stick, he shuffled over to them. "She'll take you to Lighthouse Island and back again if you treat her right. She may not look like it, but she's been on many a trip, she has."

Quigley touched the woodwork of the boat with tenderness and closed his eyes. "I called her The Seven Seas. She went on many a grand adventure. Still can feel the wind whipping me face and hear the thunder breaking overhead when I sailed her to Adventure Island." He opened his eyes and grimly smiled. "Young then. Very young." He turned and looked at himself in a half-broken mirror. "Look at me now."

"Where's Adventure Island?" Sarah asked.

"Hmm? Up the coast," Quigley replied.

"I've never heard of such a place," Will stated.

Quigley gingerly sat down on a wooden crate. "It's there all right."

Joe frowned. "But none of the maps—"

"Adventure Island isn't what the maps called it," Quigley interrupted. "Why, back then I made up me own names for all the places I went. Even that castle up on yon hill. The Haunted Castle, I called it. Quite a sight."

"What about Adventure Island?" Joe asked. "Why did you call it that?"

Quigley smiled. "Can't you guess?"

"Because you had adventures?" Sarah asked.

Quigley nodded. "When I was a lad, I went there with me best mate for several summers. We would stay there for days on end and then me father, he was a fisherman you know, would pop by with his fishing boat and pick us up. We even built our own tree house."

Joe sighed. "I wonder what our parents would say if we asked to go there."

"I don't think they would let us," Amy said. "It must be ages up the coast."

"Well, it's quite a ways," Quigley said. "I used to live in Seacrest, so I not be sure how far it is from here."

"Can we go to Lighthouse Island?" Sarah asked.

"Yes." Joe looked at Quigley. "Do you mind if we use the tools in here to fix up the sailboat?"

"Go right ahead. Those tools have been there for many a year. There should also be some spare paint lying around." Quigley stood up. "I best be getting along." He looked at Will. "Oh, and if you be wanting me to teach you how to sail—"

"Yes, please!" the children yelled excitedly.

Quigley smiled. "I'll be seeing you around then." He

turned and limped out of the shed.

Joe glanced at the others. "Do you think our parents will let us go to Lighthouse Island?"

Will nodded. "Dad will let me. After all, I've known how to swim since I was five, and the island isn't that far away."

"When can we go?" Joe asked.

"It will take a day or two to fix the boat up, and it would be good to let Quigley teach us the ropes so that we're fully prepared," Will replied. "So, we should be ready by the weekend."

~

The next day, the children arrived bright and early at the boat shed. To their joy, their parents had agreed to let them go to Lighthouse Island, but only if Quigley showed them how to sail the boat. Even though the island was nearby, anything could go wrong and, if wild weather should hit, they wanted everyone to be prepared.

The first job involved cleaning the boat. The children knew it would be dirty work, so they had worn some old clothes. Even though the boat was on a trolley with wheels, it was still hard to move. But, with the help of a fisherman, the children pulled the boat out of the shed and onto the pavement.

With buckets full of water, they began cleaning it. The old paint was partially peeling, so they needed to remove that as well. The wood needed to be nice and smooth before they put the new coat of paint on, otherwise the new paint would peel off.

It took some time but, as the hours passed, the boat began to look much improved. "Now we just need to paint her." Joe stepped back and admired his handiwork. He looked towards the paint tin that they had found. "There should be enough, but we should just paint the outside first, just in case."

"We should see if Quigley has any oars," Amy said.

"Why would we need oars?" Joe asked. "If we have the sail—"

"Amy's right," Will interrupted. "A sail is good, but what happens if there's no wind? Hopefully we won't need to use the oars, but we should have them just in case."

Will climbed into the sailboat and walked to the back where the tiller was and tested it. "It seems to work fine, but we won't know until we get it into the water."

Amy climbed aboard and peered into the little cabin. The room was pretty small and, as she stepped in, she realised she could just stand up in it. She turned and walked back to the others. "We'll be able to store the tent and other things in there if we go camping."

Will looked up at the blue sky and noticed it was perfect weather for painting since there weren't any clouds. "With the weather how it is, I say we paint now."

Joe glanced at his watch. "Why don't we go home, grab a sandwich, and return here in half an hour? We can also bring any paint brushes that we find."

~

As the three children raced up the path of Rose Cottage, they saw their mother hanging up washing on the clothesline.

"Did you get hungry?" Mrs Mitchell asked.

Joe nodded. "We came home to get something to eat, and then we're going to start painting the boat. But we only have one paintbrush, so we were wondering if you knew where we could get some more."

"Well, Mrs Thompson, the old lady who owns this cottage, did say on the phone that there was some paint in the garden shed and that we could use it if we wanted to," Mrs Mitchell said. "I imagine that there would be some brushes too."

"Thanks!" Amy yelled, rushing off towards the shed.

Their mother was right. In the far corner of the small building, they found some paint and brushes. Joe picked up four paintbrushes. "We may only need three, but I'll take four just in case."

Amy grabbed two empty tins. "If we put some paint in these, we can each have our own container of paint."

"Good idea." Joe glanced around. "Now, what else do we need?"

"I'll take these rags," Sarah said.

Joe nodded. "Okay, well, that should be all. Let's take these things to the path and leave them there while we eat some lunch."

CHAPTER 2

THE LAZY LUCY

Painting was fun. At least, that's what Amy thought as she dipped the paintbrush into the blue paint and went to work. Her arms were getting a bit sore from swishing the paint back and forth on the wood, but she didn't mind.

She stood up and admired her work. She and Sarah were painting one side of the boat, while the boys did the other side. She walked around to see how the boys were getting on. They were going a bit faster than her and Sarah, but that was because they were older. "It looks good."

"Thanks," Will said. "How's your side going?"

Before Amy could answer, thunder rumbled overhead. Looking out across the sea, she realised that storm clouds were building. "Golly! It's going to rain soon."

"Everyone stop painting!" Will ordered. "We need to get the boat back in the shed as soon as we can. Hopefully the paint will still dry in there."

While Will raced over to get a fisherman to help, the others quickly cleaned the brushes. By the time they had done this, Will had arrived back with someone. He was a strong man and, with his help, they pushed the boat back into the shed. He waved goodbye and the children gazed up at the sky as the first drops of rain fell.

Joe sighed. "We'll have to paint the rest tomorrow."

"Hey, what shall we call it?" Amy asked. "We could paint the name on the side."

Sarah nodded. "That's a great idea."

Will glanced over at the blue sailboat. "Why don't we all think of some possible names, and then tomorrow morning we can discuss them?"

"Sounds good." Amy looked at Will. "Do you feel like coming over to Rose Cottage and playing Monopoly?"

Will grinned. "Would you be able to handle it? After all, I won almost every game last time we played."

"I'm going to beat you fair and square this time." Joe opened the shed door. "Last one to Rose Cottage has to be the banker." He raced off into the driving rain.

~

The next morning, the children went straight to work on the rest of the sailboat. Once they had finished, they raced down to the sandy shore and splashed about in knee-high water as they waited for the paint to dry. It had been fun painting, but it was hot work, so it was nice to feel the cool water on their feet.

Joe collapsed onto the warm sand and closed his eyes. The others joined him and, for a few moments, no one said anything.

Sarah was the first to speak. "So, what are we going to name the boat?"

"How about Whispering Wind?" Amy suggested.

"Maybe," Joe said. "What about the Lazy Lucy?"

Will nodded. "I was thinking of something like

the Floating Four, but I do like the sound of the Lazy Lucy."

"Okay, say yes if you want to name the boat the Lazy Lucy," Joe said.

Amy and Sarah yelled out at the same time. "Yes!"

Joe looked at Will. "What do you say?"

Will thought for a moment. He then smiled. "Yes."

"Okay, so the Lazy Lucy it is," Joe said. "Now, where will our first adventure be?"

"I thought we were going to sail to Lighthouse Island," Amy said.

"Hey! I just thought of something." Will sat up and looked eagerly at the others. "Two summers ago, my father and I went camping on an island just up the coast."

"Adventure Island?" Sarah asked.

Will shook his head. "I don't think so. This place was called Windswept Island. As you might guess by the name, it was quite windy there, but there's a small cove there that was the perfect place for camping."

"Did you see many birds there?" Joe asked.

"There were quite a few, and even some wild rabbits and other small creatures," Will replied. "It's a small island, so it might not be as good if there are other people there, but when we went it was deserted."

"How far up the coast is it?" Amy questioned.

"Not far," Will replied. "A few hours, three at the most. And, if your parents agreed, we could stay there for two nights. I'm sure my father would say yes, especially since I've been there before."

"Maybe your father can talk to ours," Joe suggested.

"I'll ask him tonight," Will said. "We can still sail to Lighthouse Island if you really want to, but I think Windswept Island would be much more exciting."

Joe nodded. "I agree."

After lying on the sand for a while longer, they walked back to the boat to find that the paint was dry. They still had to attach the white sail, but before they did that, Will, in the best writing that he could muster, wrote Lazy Lucy on the side of the boat in big letters. He stood back and admired his handiwork. "There, that looks quite nice."

"Now we just need to ask Quigley for a quick lesson in sailing," Amy said.

Will nodded. "Why don't we see if he's available tomorrow?"

"Sounds smashing." Joe grinned. "Let's go and talk to him now."

As the sun neared the horizon the next day, Joe, Sarah, and Amy sat patiently at the living room table in Rose Cottage as Mr Mitchell hung up the telephone. "Well, Quigley seems to be happy with your sailing abilities, and thinks that, especially with Will in charge, nothing should go wrong. He also added that Will's experience in sailing to Windswept Island would be very helpful."

"So?" Amy asked.

Mr Mitchell grinned. "I see no reason why you can't go tomorrow—"

"Hooray!" the children yelled.

"Can we stay two nights?" Joe questioned.

"Well…" Mr Mitchell looked over at his wife. "Quigley did think very highly of them."

Their mother smiled. "If you're happy, then I'm too. Besides, it isn't like they are going to have an adventure like last time."

"Smashing!" Joe yelled.

"Goodness, thanks heaps!" Sarah shouted.

Amy hugged her mother. "Thanks a lot."

Mrs Mitchell smiled. "Just behave yourselves. And stay out of trouble."

"We will," Amy promised, smiling.

~

Early the next morning, the three siblings, with their rucksacks filled to the brim and sleeping bags slung over their shoulders, waved goodbye to their parents and headed to the harbour.

Arriving a short while later, they found that Will and Quigley were already there.

"Did you bring everything I said?" Will asked.

Joe nodded as he put his rucksack down on the ground. "Warm clothing in case the weather gets cold, some games and matches. Did you bring the tents?"

"Yes, and I've got a saucepan and bucket, and some rope," Will said.

"What about food?" Quigley asked.

"We've got tins of fruit, biscuits, bread, cocoa, chocolate, lemonade—" Amy said.

"If you're anything like me you'll be spending your time exploring," Quigley interrupted. "Why, when I explored the ruined church on Adventure Island—"

"A church?" Amy exclaimed. "On an island?"

Quigley smiled. "Yes."

"But why a church?" Joe asked, curious.

"I asked me father that same question," Quigley replied. "As far as I can recall, he said something about a religious leader, Jeremiah Jones, who wanted to start up a settlement away from the hustle and bustle of town life. He moved to the island with his followers and started building a church and a few houses."

"But you said the church was a ruin," Sarah said.

"Ah, yes," Quigley said. "Well, the story goes that Jeremiah Jones got some disease and died before he could finish building the church."

"What happened then?" Will asked.

Quigley glanced at each of the children in turn. "The followers left in a hurry, certain that the island was cursed. Some even say that, on a full moon, the ghost of Jeremiah Jones roams the island, cursing anyone in sight."

There was complete silence from the children as they digested this. Quigley, seeing the startled faces on the children, suddenly laughed. "You didn't take me seriously, did you?"

Joe smiled. "Not me. There's no such thing as a ghost."

"Well, maybe not, but it still sounded a bit frightening," Sarah said.

Quigley laughed once more as he put his hand on the little girl's shoulder. "Sorry about that. Bunch of lies I say, but I wouldn't be caught there on a full moon. Anyway, I went there plenty a time back when I was young and didn't see a sign of anyone, let alone the ghost of Jeremiah Jones. But enough of that. You're going to Windswept Island, so don't worry your pretty heads about what I say. Shall we put the boat in the water now or what?"

Will glanced around and saw several sails in the harbour that were billowing. "Yes, let's get going while the wind is still strong."

The children flung their luggage aboard the sailboat and with Quigley's help, pushed the craft down the slope. It slid into the water with a splash.

The children clambered in. Waving goodbye to Quigley, Will took the tiller and the Lazy Lucy headed out of the cove.

It was a marvellous morning as the boat whipped along the coast. While Will took charge of the tiller, the girls gazed up at the blue sky. Whenever a cloud came along, they would try to imagine it as an animal.

With the binoculars around his neck, Joe sat at the stern of the boat. Every now and then he would let his hand drag in the water to cool himself off.

Seeing the billowing sail, Joe marvelled at how such a simple thing could propel the sailboat at the speed that they were going. At this rate, they were sure to reach Windswept Island before midday.

And indeed they did a short while later. "Land ahoy!" Joe gazed at Windswept Island. It didn't look particularly interesting since it was flat, but he didn't care. As long as there were birds, he'd be happy.

Will steered the Lazy Lucy towards the island. As they got closer, they saw some large sea birds flying over the rocks. Nearer to the inlet, the smiles on the children's faces dropped as they heard music.

"Where's the music coming from?" Amy asked.

Will steered the boat into the inlet and came into sight of a group of campers tenting in the sheltered area. Several people were jumping up and down as they danced to loud music.

"Looks like somebody beat us to it," Will muttered, annoyed.

"They must have a gramophone," Sarah said.

Joe peered through the binoculars. "Sarah's right."

Will looked at the faces of the others and saw how disappointed they looked. "I'm sorry."

"Can we camp somewhere else?" Amy asked.

"Well, this island is quite small, so that's the only place to camp," Will replied.

Joe glanced wistfully at the birds flying overhead. "What a shame."

"So what do we do?" Sarah questioned.

"Well, let's see where we are." Will went into the cabin and returned a moment later with a map. He laid it out and pointed. "We're here. If you want, we could go back to Lighthouse Island."

"What about this island here?" Joe asked as he pointed to another island further up the coast. "Would that be Adventure Island?"

Will looked closer and saw that the name of it was Rocky Island. He shook his head. "I don't think so. I think this other place would be the one that Quigley was talking about." He pointed to an island a fair distance past Rocky. "This one is closest to Seacrest, which is where Quigley used to live, so I think that would probably be Adventure Island."

Amy glanced at her watch. "If this wind keeps up, we could make Rocky Island by late afternoon, right?"

Will studied the distances between Windswept Island and Smugglers Cove and Windswept Island and Rocky Island. "Rocky Island is about double the distance from Smugglers as Windswept is, but if we have the same weather conditions as we had earlier, we should get there by late afternoon."

"Let's get some food in our stomachs before we head off," Joe suggested.

Will looked at the girls. "So, are we all in agreement?"

Sarah grinned. "Aye, aye, Captain."

Amy smiled "Whatever you say, Captain."

"Okay, here we come Rocky Island!" Will yelled, thrusting his hand into the air.

CHAPTER 3

ROCKY ISLAND

Before long, the Lazy Lucy was once more whipping along the coast. The sail billowed out fully and the boat bobbed up and down on the water as it sped along. But then the wind died down and there was nothing that they could do about it. They took the sail down and rowed, but progress was slow.

Thankfully, the wind picked up and, after raising the sail, the Lazy Lucy sped along the water. As late afternoon came to a close, land came into view.

Will, who was now resting while Joe steered, was the first to spot it. "Rocky Island dead ahead!" He walked over and took the tiller from Joe. "The island probably got its name because of all the rocks, so we'd better go slowly and keep a sharp look out for anything that could damage the boat."

Everyone was silent as the craft got closer to the island. Soon, they were within sight of the rocks. The waves frothed and surged as the water crashed against them, sending spray high into the air.

"We should take down the sail," Will suggested. "I think it's best if we row from this point on. We want to have control of the direction we are going in. If the Lazy Lucy hits one of the rocks—"

"I'm on it, Captain," Joe interrupted, walking over to dismantle the sail.

With Sarah watching for rocks on one side and Amy on the other, Will and Joe took the oars and started rowing.

Whenever the boat got too close to one of the rocks, the watcher would yell out and Will would adjust the direction. It was slow going, and the boys had to row for roughly ten minutes before they found a way through the rocks.

As the Lazy Lucy entered the small inlet and headed towards the sandy beach, Amy shared a glance with the others. "That was tight."

"How about we drop the anchor next to those flat rocks?" Will suggested. "That will save us wading through the water."

"Good thinking," Joe replied.

They brought the boat alongside the rocks. Will slung the anchor overboard and climbed out, gazing around as he did so. The tall cliffs made it impossible to see much of the island.

"We should have time to explore before it gets dark," Amy said.

"Yes, but we should set up camp first." Will glanced around at the surrounding area. "Why don't you girls look around and see if there's a suitable place to camp? We boys can get the tents and stuff out of the boat and onto the beach."

The two girls jumped down onto the rocks and made their way across to the beach while the boys started unloading the gear. They had just finished doing so when the girls came rushing back.

"Did you find a spot?" Joe asked.

Sarah nodded. "A good one."

"There's a sheltered spot in front of a wooded area,"

Amy said. "The grass seems nice and soft and, if we aim the tents the right way, we'll have the morning sun waking us up."

"Sounds good," Will said. "Let's get going." After picking up their stuff, they walked along the sand and headed up the hillside.

After a few minutes, they arrived at the grassy area. Everyone went straight to work and, before long, two small tents were set up beside a wood of pines and birches. After they had grabbed some firewood, they decided to explore.

They walked alongside the woods as they headed towards a hill that seemed to be in the middle of the island. With the pines on one side and thick gorse bushes on the other, it was a lovely walk.

Sarah was thrilled when she saw a couple of wild rabbits dart across the grass. "Oh, what sweet little darlings!"

As they reached the hill and started walking up it, they caught sight of a stream. Upon further inspection, they saw that the water was coming out of some rocks.

"This will provide us with fresh water, to drink or wash the dishes," Will said.

"I wonder what else we'll find," Joe said, racing up the hill.

The others followed him and, before long, they were at the rocky top. There were a few trees as well as stunted gorse bushes which was due to the rocky terrain.

Amy gazed around. "You can see the whole island from here." Unlike most small islands, there was quite a large wooded area. There were also grassy areas, especially near the rocky shoreline.

Soon, all eyes were on one spot. For some reason, there was a square in the middle of the woods that was devoid of trees. And, in the middle of this square was some sort of ruin.

The children couldn't see what it was from so far away, so they decided to go and have a look. They hurried down the hill, through the woods and into the clearing.

They stopped when they saw the ruin. Amy looked at the boys. "Are you thinking what I'm thinking?"

Joe walked forward. "It couldn't be."

The others followed and soon they were so close to the ruined building that there was no doubt about it.

It was a church. Inscribed on a piece of wood that was half rotted away was a sign. It read: The Church of Jeremiah Jones.

Amy gasped. "Golly! So this is Adventure Island."

"Oh, no!" Sarah exclaimed. "If the church is real, then the curse is real."

Will shook his head. "No. A church is one thing, a ghost another."

"I want to go home," Sarah muttered.

Joe glanced up at the sky. "Even if we wanted to go home, it would be too late. Besides, who really believes in ghosts?"

The boys laughed and, a few moments later, the girls joined in. Joe walked into the ruined building and saw that the years had taken their toll on the structure. Weeds and bushes were climbing through windows and holes in the walls.

"This sure has been here a while," Will said.

"I wonder why they don't do something about this place," Amy muttered.

"Who would want to live on this island anyway?" Joe questioned. "Besides, the government probably owns the island now."

They left the church and glanced around at their

surroundings. There were a few other ruined buildings that looked in as bad a shape as the church and Joe assumed that they would have been the houses that the religious leader had been building. The only other building that was worth exploring was located beside the church. It was large place, almost as big as the church.

"It looks like a warehouse," Sarah said.

They went inside and saw that most of it was still intact. The sides were made of stone while an upper level was rotting away as it was made of timber. In places, they could even see the sky above.

"This must have been a storehouse of some kind," Will said. "After all, if these people were going to be living here, they wouldn't want to be going back and forth to the mainland all the time to get food. And, with the walls being stone, the food would stay cool."

Leaving the storehouse, the children walked out into the open. "I wonder why Quigley liked this island so much," Sarah said.

"There must be something else to explore," Will replied. "After all, Quigley did say that he came here several times and loved it."

Amy looked up at the sky. "We'd better get back to camp. I don't want to be here when darkness falls."

"Me neither," Sarah replied as she followed her sister towards the campsite.

On the way back, the girls collected some heather to put under their sleeping bags while the boys gathered some dry sticks to use as firewood.

~

As night set in, the boys started a fire. Soon, the dry wood started to crackle and, every now and then, the flames would flare up and light up the surrounding area just that little bit more.

"That was a delicious meal," Amy said as she finished eating the soup that had been heated up on the fire.

Will handed out the steaming cups. "Here's some hot cocoa to wash it all down."

As Amy sipped her drink, she glanced up at the dark sky. All that could be seen was a full moon. She glanced at the others. "Hey, what about the curse?"

Joe looked up at the sky and saw the moon. "It does look like a full moon, but I wouldn't worry. Just because some old guy said something—"

"But he was right about the church," Sarah interrupted.

Will looked at the girls. "Quigley is getting old, and with old age some people tend to forget things and mix fact with fiction. So, just because he was right about the church doesn't mean that he was right about the ghost. We all know that ghosts don't exist."

"If you're scared—" Joe said.

"I'm not scared." Amy looked at Sarah. "Are you?"

"No," Sarah replied, putting on a brave face.

"Now that we've got that settled, who wants to play a game of snap?" Will said.

The moon was high in the sky when Sarah, awakened by a strange noise, sat up. She listened intently but didn't hear anything. She started to lie back down, but then heard the noise once again. She sat back up and shook her sister. "Amy, wake up."

"Go back to sleep," Amy mumbled, half asleep.

Suddenly, both girls heard a ghostly laugh. Amy, now fully awake, sat up. "The boys. They must be playing a trick on us to make us scared."

"You don't think it's a real ghost?" Sarah asked.

"Of course not. I'll show you." Amy crawled to the end of the tent. She glanced over at the boy's tent and saw a light flickering. "There, I told you. They're both awake." She grinned. "Why don't we make some noises and scare the boys?"

Sarah smiled. "Okay."

The two girls crawled out of their tent and crept over to the boys tent. Then, when they were right outside the flap, Amy and Sarah started making ghostly noises.

"This is Jeremiah Jones, and I'm coming to get you," Amy said in the ghostliest voice that she could think of. She tapped on the tent. "I'm a coming, I'm a coming, I'm a coming."

Sarah reached forward and started to open the flap on the tent.

Both girls nearly burst out laughing as they heard the scared voices of the boys as they whispered amongst themselves.

Amy got a stick and poked it through the tent flap. "I'm a..." Suddenly the stick was grabbed from the inside and she fell forward into the tent. When she sat up, she saw the grinning faces of the boys in front of her.

"Did you really think you could fool us?" Will questioned.

"We weren't scared one bit," Joe stated.

"I heard you whispering," Sarah said, entering the tent.

"We were play acting. Isn't that right?" Joe said, looking at Will.

Will nodded. "Of course. We had to act as though we were scared. But did you really think we could be scared by a bunch of ghostly noises?"

"Why did you try it on us then?" Sarah asked.

Joe frowned. "What are you talking about?"

Amy stared at the boys. "The first lot of noises. They were you, right?"

Suddenly, a loud ghostly sound broke the silence. Everyone yelled out in fright. Sarah scrambled inside the tent and pulled the flap closed. They all huddled at the back of the tent, cramped and scared. As the seconds passed and they heard no more noises, the boys started to relax.

"There's no such thing as ghosts, so why are we getting all worked up?" Joe said.

"Then what made that noise?" Amy asked.

"Some kind of animal," Will stated with more confidence than he actually felt.

Sarah froze at the sound of more noises. "What kind of animal?"

A ghostly voice suddenly yelled out. "I am Jeremiah Jones, and you are on my island. And tonight is a full moon."

"It must be someone playing a trick on us," Joe said.

"What about Quigley?" Amy suggested.

"Of course!" Will exclaimed. "Though, how did he know we were going to Rocky Island?"

"I don't know, but I'm going to see if there's a face with this voice." Joe took his torch and crawled to the flap. He glanced back. "Are you coming or not?"

All four of them crawled out of the tent and stood up on the grass as the noises stopped. In front of them were the dying embers of the fire. It was a clear sky and the full moon shone brightly.

No one could be seen. No animal and no person.

Joe shone the torch from side to side. "Whatever it was, they must…" He paused as the torchlight picked up a ghostly figure.

The children froze. He, if it was a he, was dressed in a flowing white cape.

The ghost yelled out. "I am Jeremiah Jones. If you are not gone by midnight tomorrow, I will return and put a curse on you that will last forever. So get off my island!"

Suddenly, there was a puff of smoke that covered the area. When it drifted away, the ghost was no longer there.

CHAPTER 4

JEREMIAH JONES

"Where did he go?" Joe hurried forward and shone the torch around. No one could be seen.

The children listened for the next few moments, but nothing could be heard.

"I want to go home tomorrow," Sarah cried out.

"Wait!" Joe said. "Just because something that looked like a ghost—"

"He was a ghost," Sarah interrupted. "Did we hear him come? No. Did we hear him go? No. If you think I am going to stay any longer on this island, you must be crazy."

"Just because you're scared—" Joe shouted.

"Hold on everyone," Will interrupted. "Let's just all calm down. Why don't we go back to sleep, try to get a good rest, and talk in the morning? There's nothing we can do tonight, so let's think our decision over."

"Well, okay," Sarah said.

The sun shone brightly and the seagulls were circling overhead the next morning as the children ate breakfast. Even a few rabbits could be seen hopping around on the grass.

After finishing off a tin of peaches, Sarah glanced around at everyone. "When are we going to leave?"

"Why don't we have a vote?" Joe suggested. "Put your hand up if you want to stay." He and Will raised their hands. "Okay, and now put up your hand if you want to go."

Amy and Sarah put up their hands.

Joe stared down at the fire. "Ghosts do not exist, full stop."

"Well, whatever thing we saw last night, it looked pretty real to me," Sarah protested.

"Me too," Amy said.

"What if it was a person dressed up?" Joe suggested. "Just suppose that someone dressed up and pretended to be that religious fellow to scare us off this island."

"And why would they do that?" Amy questioned.

"I don't know," Joe admitted, "but I want to find out."

Amy glanced at Sarah, then back at Joe. "I'll give you until noon to prove your theory, okay?"

Joe looked at Will. "If that ghost is a fake, we'll be able to find some evidence."

Will nodded. "Let's go and search."

The children headed to the church which was where the boys wanted to search first. Upon reaching the ruin, they split up and searched the area, looking for anything that might indicate that there was someone else on the island. But they couldn't find anything.

"There doesn't seem to be anything here," Amy said as she stood in front of the church.

"But I'm telling you, there are no such things as…" Joe paused as he heard a ghostly wail.

A moment later, a ghostly voice shouted out. "Why are you still here?"

Will looked around but he couldn't see anyone. He entered the church, but as the voice shouted out again, he realised it wasn't coming from there. Stepping out, he followed the others to the storehouse.

Amy shouted out as she saw a white figure in front of the lone window near the roof of the building. "Look!"

The others peered up but couldn't see anything. As the ghostly voice fell silent, they questioned Amy.

"What did you see?" Joe asked.

"Something white," Amy stammered. "It was some-one or something."

"Did you see a face?" Will questioned.

Amy shook her head. "It was too quick. But there was nothing human about it." She pointed to the window. "It was right there."

Leaving the girls standing outside, the boys entered the storehouse and looked up. "What do you think?" Joe whispered.

Will looked up at the rotting timber roof above them, but no one could be seen. However, there was one spot directly next to the window that had not rotted away, and it was possible someone could have been hiding there. Will walked further into the building as he tried to find a ladder. But none could be seen.

Joe pointed to the left hand corner of the storehouse. "If we had a ladder, we could place it up against that end."

The ghost yelled out again. "Come midnight and you will be cursed forever! Get off my island! This is my last warning!"

Joe turned to Will. "Let's get back to the girls before they get too scared." As they headed back, he spotted something on the ground. He picked it up. It was a cigarette butt. One that had not been there for long. He showed it to Will. "Look."

A grin spread across Will's face. "Gosh! There must be a person up there."

"But how do we prove it?" Joe asked.

"I've got a plan. Just follow my lead." Will led the way out of the storehouse and found the girls huddled together behind a rock.

"Did you find anything?" Sarah asked.

Will shook his head. "No, let's go home."

"I never want to come here again," Joe said.

Amy looked shocked. "What? But you just said—"

"I was wrong," Joe interrupted. "Come on, let's go. Just standing here is giving me the creeps."

As the two boys hurried towards the hill, Amy shot a glance at Sarah. "What just happened?"

"I don't know, but I'm happy to be going back. Come on, last one to reach the boys has to make lunch." Sarah sprinted off after the boys.

~

By the time the children arrived back at the campsite, the girls knew the story behind the boy's weird actions as they had told them everything.

The girls may have been scared by a ghost, but if it was a person, which the boys were certain it was, that meant that someone was trying to scare them away. And, if someone was trying to scare them away they probably had something to hide.

"The man might still be watching us, so we have to pretend we're leaving the island," Will said.

"And then what?" Amy asked.

"We'll row around the island until we find another place to hide the boat," Will replied. "Then, after we have set up camp somewhere else, we'll see if we can find out what's going on."

The children packed up their stuff and headed down the path to the beach. After they had put everything on board, they set off.

Will and Joe took the oars while the girls kept a lookout. They didn't want to hoist the sail since they would be going close to dangerous rocks and, if the sail was up, the boat would only go the way of the wind, and thus might smash against the rocks.

There were a few tense moments as the boys rowed out of the inlet, but soon they were out on calm water.

Will stopped rowing for a moment and scanned the horizon as the Lazy Lucy bobbed to and fro on the water. "We'll head left. There should be fewer rocks on the side closest to the mainland, but keep your eyes open."

"For rocks or the ghost?" Joe asked.

"For both." Will steered the Lazy Lucy towards the mainland. "Most likely, the person is camped on the other side of the island where we haven't been yet. So we shouldn't go too far."

"What about here?" Sarah asked as she pointed towards the shore.

Will looked over and saw a small section of sand and, next to it, a half-flooded cave. An idea crept into his mind. "Yes, that might work."

"What do you mean?" Joe asked.

Will glanced at his watch. "It's high tide now, and that cave looks deep enough to sail into."

"But if it's high tide now, what happens at low tide?" Amy questioned.

"Well, the Lazy Lucy would be beached on the sand. But that will be okay. We just need to keep her out of view of anyone on this island." Will peered towards the sharp rocks that bordered the cave. "It's going to be tight, but I think we can just squeeze in there."

Amy moved up to the front of the boat. "I'll be the lookout out front."

There was a ring of rocks around the cave, with only one opening. It was going to be touch and go. And they had to be fast. Any slowdown on speed and the boat would drift to the left or right, which would put it on course for the rocks.

The four children shouted out to one another as the Lazy Lucy headed towards the frothing waters.

"All clear this side!" Sarah shouted.

"You're fine to go straight ahead," Amy yelled.

"Let's do it." Will pulled as hard as he could on the oars.

The Lazy Lucy surged forward as it bobbed up and down on the waves, getting closer and closer to the opening. Closer, closer, and closer, and then they were through.

"Yes!" Sarah yelled, happy. She turned to Will and smiled.

Suddenly, the boat groaned, and the sound of breaking of wood filled the air. Sarah glanced down and saw that a rock had torn a small hole in the side of the boat.

"Oh no!" Sarah shouted. "There's a hole in the boat! We're all going to drown!"

CHAPTER 5

THE DISAPPEARING MAN

Joe stared as water started pouring in the Lazy Lucy. "Blow! What are we going to do?"

"Just hold on and pray that we don't hit anything else," Will yelled. Along with Joe, he rowed towards the cave and, a few moments later, the sailboat was successfully hidden from the outside.

This was one problem solved, but they still had another problem to deal with, which was the water still pouring into the boat.

Will hurried into the cabin and glanced around for something with which to bail out the water that was already filling the bottom of the small room. It would soon reach the tins of food that were tucked inside the little cupboard. This wasn't so much of a problem since they were waterproof, but not so for the tents, books, and clothes that were just above the food.

Will grabbed two plastic bowls and hurried back. He handed them to the girls. "Get to work." He turned to Joe. "Come with me."

As the girls set to work getting as much of the water out as possible, the boys removed everything from the cabin and put it on the roof. The water slowly rose higher and higher. Soon, all of the children's shoes were soaking wet.

As Will finished removing everything from the cabin, he realised that the boat was no longer sinking. He quickly grabbed one of the poles from the tent and poked it into the water beside the boat.

He grinned as the pole struck bottom roughly two feet down. "Hey! The sand's just below us." He looked over at the girls who were still furiously tossing the water out. "You can stop now."

"What? Why?" Amy asked.

"The water will keep on coming in until the level in the boat is at the same level in the cave. And we've moved all the stuff out of harms way, so come and join us." Will walked over to the cabin and climbed up onto the roof.

The others quickly followed and, for the next minute or two, they watched the water slowly rise. As Will had predicted, once the water had risen to the same level as in the cave, it stopped flowing in.

"So, what do we do now?" Sarah asked.

"Well, we can wait for the water to go down, or we can jump in now and dry ourselves out by the beach," Will replied.

"How deep did you say it was?" Amy questioned.

"Well, it was two feet at one point, but it could be deeper or shallower somewhere else." Will looked down at the foaming water. "I'll test it." After rolling up his trousers, he climbed down into the boat. Climbing over the side, he lowered himself into the water. He smiled as the water reached his knees. "Looks good here. I'll see how it is getting to the sand."

The others watched as Will slowly walked through the water and saw that it gradually became shallower. Within half a minute, he was on the dry sand. He turned and walked back through the water. "Deepest part is the start. Just walk where I walked. There's no telling what will happen to you if you stray offline, so stay straight."

Following Will's advice, the others waded into the water. Before long, and without any trouble, all four of them were sitting on the hot sand. However, the tents and other essentials had to be collected and so, leaving their shoes to dry in the sun, they headed back into the water.

Forming a chain, they were able to quickly get all of their stuff off the Lazy Lucy. After having a short rest, they lugged the tents across the beach and up the rugged terrain.

"We need to be close to the boat, but not too close," Will said. "We can't afford to be seen from the water, so I suggest we get as close to the woods as possible."

They walked a bit farther on until they reached the woods and, seeing a patch of grass, dropped the tents there.

Joe glanced around and saw that the woods blocked the view at one end, and thick gorse bushes blocked the view from the beach. "This should suit us nicely."

"Let's hurry and set up camp," Amy said. "I want to see if there's something more to your theory than just a cigarette butt."

It didn't take as long to set up camp as it had yesterday and, after a quick snack, they headed towards the church. They kept close to the wood at all times and stopped when they were in view of the ruin.

Will looked through the binoculars but, to his disappointment, didn't see any movement. "I vote we stay in the shelter of the bushes and head for the other end of the island."

Since it seemed pointless staying where they were, the others agreed with Will and moved off. It took less than ten minutes to reach the far beach and, in the shelter of thick bushes, the children lay down and gazed down the small incline at the sand below.

Joe took the binoculars and spent a full minute surveying the area. There was still no sign of anyone and not even a sign that anyone had been there in recent times. There was no boat, no tent, not even a campfire.

Sarah stood up. "This is no mystery. How can there be one when there isn't anyone or anything of interest on this island?"

Joe watched as Sarah started walking down the small hill and towards the beach. "I guess she's right." He stood up as well. "Why are we all creeping about?"

"Look!" Amy called out. She pointed to the far end of the beach where a person had just come into view.

"Gosh, they'll see Sarah." Will jumped up and rushed after the eight year old.

Joe and Amy watched in horrified silence as the man walked down the beach, heading directly towards Sarah who, by now, had just reached the sand. Luckily though, there was a rocky cliff that protruded out and thus stopped the man from seeing the girl.

With bated breath, Joe gazed through the binoculars as Will caught up with Sarah. The two of them turned and raced back to the grassy area. They had just flung themselves behind some gorse bushes when the man walked around the cliff and headed towards them.

"What's going on?" Amy asked.

"The man must have seen them. He's going straight... no, he's turned around now and... he's disappeared!" Joe whipped the binoculars away from his face and gazed down at the beach. He was right. The man had literally disappeared.

Half a minute later, Will and Sarah rejoined the

others. The boy turned to Joe. "What did you see?"

"You were just in time," Joe said. "I thought the man had seen you, but then he disappeared."

Will frowned. "What do you mean?"

"He just disappeared," Joe replied. "He was—"

"Goodness, the cave!" Sarah whispered.

"What cave?" Amy asked.

"Just before Will spoke to me, I saw a cave," Sarah explained.

Joe looked at Will. "Did you see it?"

Will shook his head. "No, but I wasn't looking."

"Remember the caves at Smuggles Cove?" Joe said. "What if there are similar caves on this island?"

"Caves would be an ideal hiding place for someone who didn't want to be seen." Amy glanced at Will. "Are there many caves that you know of in the area?"

Will nodded. "This part of the coast was a big deal to smugglers a few hundred years ago. It was a perfect distance from France, so smugglers spent many a day building tunnels. There are even rumours that Smugglers Cove was built on top of a network of tunnels."

"You mean the ones we found?" Sarah asked.

Will shook his head. "No. According to some of the stories, what we found only amounts to a fraction of what there is. So, yes, it's certainly possible that there are caves on this island."

Joe stood up. "Let's explore them. If there's something going on, I'm sure there must be something in those tunnels." He scanned the beach. No one could be seen. "We know there is at least one person around, so stay alert."

"What happens if we're seen?" Amy asked.

"We'll pretend we're four children out sailing," Joe replied.

CHAPTER 6

INTO THE CAVES

The children walked down the hill going as quietly as they could. Stepping onto the soft sand, they saw that Sarah had been right. A cave lay just to the right of them. Waiting for a moment to make sure that no one was about, the children entered.

It was dark inside, so much so that they needed to turn on their torches. The beams of light shone around the dark space. They spotted nothing of interest. It looked like any other rocky cave, nothing out of the ordinary.

Will flicked his torch around the walls as he walked close to them in an effort to see if there was a tunnel. But there was none. It didn't take long for the children to group back together at the entrance.

"Well, there's nothing in there," Joe said, disappointed. "I felt sure that there would be something."

"But what about the man?" Amy asked. "Where did he disappear to?"

Sarah glanced further along and saw that there was another cave a short distance away. "Maybe he went in there."

Will nodded. "Let's search."

They hurried over and were soon in the cave which

was double the size of the previous one. Like all the others, Joe was very familiar with caves, especially after their last adventure and, as he felt the rocky wall, he hoped to discover a tunnel. But no rocks gave way and nothing seemed out of the ordinary.

Amy yelled out as she picked up something that was on the cave floor and held it up. "Look what I've found."

The others raced over and Joe saw it was another cigarette butt. "How long do you think that has been here?"

"It doesn't look too old. Not longer than a few days." Will glanced around. "As there's no tunnel, whoever is on the island isn't staying in this cave." He walked out of the cave and onto the sand. As the others joined him, he looked around. There were a few gulls in the sky above, but that was all. He looked towards the trees at the far end of the inlet. There were quite a few, enough to hide a building. "Why don't we walk towards the woods over there and see if we can see anything?"

"Sounds like a good plan," Joe said.

The four of them walked along the beach as they headed to the other side of the island. They were about halfway there when Amy suddenly stopped. She raised her hand and pointed to the trees in front of them. "Is that a person?"

Will raised his binoculars to his eyes and peered through them. "Yes. It's a man."

"What does he look like?" Joe questioned.

"He's bald and tall." Will looked back at the others for a moment. "Was the man you saw near the cave bald?"

Joe shook his head. "No."

"What's he doing now?" Amy asked.

Will looked back through the binoculars. After gazing around for one minute, he dropped the binoculars, disappointed.

"Has he gone?" Joe asked.

Will nodded. "He must have headed deeper into the woods."

"Maybe if we hurry we can catch sight of him," Sarah suggested.

"Possibly." Will raced along the sand, fuelled by the desire to catch up to the man. They were soon standing at the edge of the woods. Will walked to where he had seen the man.

"What was the man doing?" Amy asked.

"He was looking around," Will replied. "Almost as though he didn't want anyone to see where he was going."

"I wonder why?" Joe asked.

"Let's see if we can find where he went." Will led the others into the woods. There wasn't much of a path, just an animal track. The track meandered along, sometimes getting quite close to the rocky cliffs, but always staying within the confines of the woods.

Will was just about to suggest that they turn back when something caught his attention. He shot his hand up. "Quiet! I see something."

Sarah frowned as she peered forward and saw a small log cabin. "Do you think the man went in there?"

"It seems like a good possibility." Will crept forward, going from the trunk of one tree to the next, pausing each time as he did so. But, apart from some birds chirping, all was silent.

From what Amy could see, there was only one window on this side of the cabin. She assumed that the door and possibly another window would be on the other. She joined the others at the corner of the cabin. "Are we going to look through the window?"

Joe surveyed the dirty window. "I'm not sure how much I'll be able to see, but get ready to run in case someone's in there."

The air was tense with anticipation as Joe hugged the cabin wall and sidled towards the window. He paused once he was right next to it and, after glancing back to make sure that nothing had happened to the others, he looked through the glass.

The moss and grime that covered the lower half of the windowpane made it hard to get a clear view of the inside, but Joe saw enough to satisfy him. He turned and walked back to the others.

"Is anyone there?" Will asked.

"Not that I can see, but someone has definitely been there," Joe replied.

"Why?" Amy questioned. "What did you see?"

"There are some sleeping bags, some food—" Joe replied.

"How many sleeping bags?" Will interrupted.

"At least two, maybe three. But I..." Joe paused as the bushes nearby rustled.

"Maybe we should talk somewhere else," Sarah said.

Suddenly, a large bird flew up from the bushes.

"Phew! It's only a bird." Joe glanced at the others. "I'll just see if the door's unlocked, and then we'll go."

"But what if someone comes?" Amy asked, worried.

"Hope that they don't." Joe hurried around to the other side of the cabin and paused at the door. He reached for the handle and turned it. It swung open without a sound. The hinges had clearly been oiled. That, as well as the sleeping bags, confirmed that someone had been living in here for a period of time.

Joe waved to the others and they hurried over. They all glanced around the small cabin. There were a couple of sleeping bags, some tins of food, a small table, and two chairs. There were also three rucksacks leaning against the wall.

Joe walked over to them and was just about to open one to see what was inside when the sound of voices reached his ears. Standing up, he looked back at the others. "Do you hear that?"

"We have to go!" Amy whispered.

All four of them ran as fast as they could through the woods in the opposite direction from where the voices were coming from. It was an anxious few moments until they reached the some thick bushes.

Peering through the foliage, they saw three men come into view. They were still talking, but it wasn't loud enough for the children to hear what was being said. They entered the cabin and closed the door.

The children waited for a few minutes to see if they would come out, but when they didn't, they decided to head back to the beach.

After making sure they couldn't be seen through the cabin windows, they made their way back along the path and, before long, were on the beach. They sat down and rested on the sand as they thought about what they had just seen.

"So, why do you think those men are here?" Amy asked.

"It could be any number of reasons," Joe replied.

"One of them must have dressed up as a ghost and tried to scare us," Will said.

"But why?" Sarah asked. "What possible reason could they have for staying on this island?"

"I don't know. I truly don't." Will frowned as he caught sight of the men as they emerged from the woods. "Oh, no! We need to hide!" He stood up, but paused as one of the men turned and saw him.

CHAPTER 7

THE BIRDWATCHERS

As the men approached, Will quickly whispered to the others. "Don't let them know that we suspect anything. Just follow my lead."

The others had just enough time to nod before the bald man called out. "Hey! What are you doing here?"

"We're camping," Will said.

"We can't have visitors on this island, so you'll have to move off," the bald man said.

"What about you?" Joe asked. "Why are you on this island then?"

"We're doing a very important study for the government about the bird population in this area," the bald man replied.

Amy studied the three men. They were rough looking and were untidily dressed. "You don't look like government people."

The bald man looked at the children in turn. "What would your parents say if they knew you were interfering with the government? I don't think they would be too pleased."

"We're not doing anything wrong," Sarah piped up.

The man sneered. "You kids are all the same. Why, I wouldn't be surprised if you've been snooping on us.

Haven't you heard about the ghost that haunts this island?"

"Jeremiah Jones?" Joe asked.

The man nodded. "Yes, so I wouldn't stay any longer on this island if I were you."

"But you're staying here," Amy said.

"That's different. It's our job," the bald man replied. "We can't leave. But if you stay here tonight, I'm sure you'll be visited by the ghost and who knows what will happen. So leave this island as soon as you can." He gazed at the four children before he turned and walked away. The other men followed him.

Once they were out of hearing distance, Sarah looked towards Joe. "What if the ghost does come again?"

Joe laughed. "They were just trying to scare us."

"But we did see the ghost," Amy stated.

"It was one of those men dressed up," Joe said. "I know we don't have proof, but there are no such things as ghosts. However, we can see whether or not the men are lying about being birdwatchers." He turned to Will. "Do you know much about the birds that live around here?"

"Yes, why?" Will questioned.

As Joe led the way down the hill half an hour later and walked over to where the three men were standing below a tall pine tree, he saw that they had changed into cleaner clothes. One of them, the bald fellow who had spoken to them earlier, was now wearing a nametag on his chest. It read: Marvin – Bird Researcher.

Joe turned to the man. "Have you seen the Dodo yet?"

Marvin hesitated. "I'm not sure." He looked over at the man standing next to him who had a ponytail and wore glasses. "Have you, Luke?"

Luke shook his head. "Of course we haven't. They're extinct. Besides, they lived in Africa." He gazed at Joe. "You mustn't know a lot about birds, boy."

"What about a Grey Wagtail?" Sarah asked. "We just saw one last week in Smugglers Cove."

"Did you now?" Luke said. "Well, I think we saw one here the other day, didn't we, Kenneth?"

The third man, a short, thin fellow with beady eyes, nodded. "Yes, just near those hills." He pointed to the hillside that the children had just walked down.

"Was he grey and red or grey and blue?" Joe asked. "The one we saw was grey and blue."

Kenneth looked to Luke. "I can't recall. Which one do you think it was?"

Luke paused as he thought. "It was grey and blue, just like yours."

Joe nodded. "Well, we had better get going. Oh, and we've decided to leave this afternoon."

"I'm glad you've got some sense in you," Marvin stated.

"We thought about what you said about the ghost and decided we had better not be here at nightfall," Joe said.

Marvin smiled. "Quite right. Well, have a good trip home."

"We will. Bye." Joe turned and walked away, the others following close behind.

As soon as the children had reached the top of the hill, they stopped and, hiding behind a bush, peered through the leaves.

As Joe saw the men leave the trees and head in the direction of the beach, he glanced at the others. "It worked. They're going back to the cabin."

"They'll probably change back into their other clothes right away," Amy said.

Will nodded. "Yes, now that they think that we're going home."

"But we're not," Joe stated. "And all because of the Grey Wagtail."

"It was a good thing we had two birds in mind," Sarah said.

"Yes. They surprised me with the Dodo, so it was either a lucky guess or they do know some stuff, but they did what I thought they would when the Grey Wagtail was mentioned." Joe chuckled. "If only they knew that it was grey and yellow."

"There's still a chance that they are telling the truth," Amy said. "After all, not every birdwatcher could possibly know every type of bird."

"Well, no, but there are too many things that are not making sense," Joe said. "I suggest we explore the island from end to end. We could uncover something that will explain why the men are here."

"Shall we search the middle of the island or the shoreline first?" Will asked.

"Shoreline. We can go back to camp, have a quick meal, and then search." Joe walked towards the woods, which would take them back to the campsite.

The children strolled along the beach where the caves were and stayed on the edge of the woods as the shoreline became more jagged and dangerous looking.

Waves pounded the area and, as they rounded a corner, everyone stopped as they caught sight of a lighthouse. Sitting at the end of a row of rocks that jutted out to sea, it looked as though it would be a hair-raising experience to get to the building.

"I wonder why we didn't see this from the hill," Amy said.

"We were too distracted with the church," Will said. "Besides, it doesn't look as though it's still operating. It probably closed down when they built the new one on Lighthouse Island. After all, this may have been built more than a hundred years ago, so I'm not sure what condition it would be in now."

They were silent for a moment as they watched a wave break over the rocks in the middle. Joe looked at his watch. "If we came here when it was low tide, we would be able to hop over the rocks."

"But if it's deserted, I don't see much point," Amy said as she gazed out at the towering structure. "Hey, I wonder if we could call for help using the lamp." After taking the binoculars from Will, she put them to her eyes and looked at the lamp room.

"What can you see?" Sarah asked.

"Some of the windows are cracked in parts, and the lamp also looks to be cracked, so I would be very surprised if it still worked." Amy let the binoculars hang around her neck. "Well, we can't cross now even if we wanted to, so let's move on."

Leaving the noise of the crashing waves behind them, the children walked along the shoreline where there were fewer rocks and the water was much calmer.

After seeing nothing of interest, they decided to explore inland for a bit and, while they were walking past some trees, Joe caught sight of some birds on the ground.

They flew upwards and Joe followed them with his eyes up into the trees. He paused as something caught his eye. "Hey, look up there."

The others looked up and saw that high above, in the branches of a massive oak tree, was a tree house.

"Golly," Amy said. "Is that the tree house that Quigley made?"

Will shook his head. "I doubt it. The wood would have rotted away by now."

Sarah stared at the tree trunk. "Look, there are pieces of wood attached to the tree."

"That must be how you get up to it." Will walked forward and started climbing. The others watched on as he went past the first three pieces of wood. As he stepped onto the fourth one, it broke away from the tree.

CHAPTER 8

A STRANGER IN NEED

The others looked on anxiously as Will steadied himself. "Are you okay?" Amy asked.

Will nodded. "But I'd better come down now."

"It's a pity that happened." Joe looked up at the tree house. "That would have been a good place to hide from the men."

From what Joe could see, some of the timber had rotted away and, as he walked around the tree, he saw that there were only a few planks of wood remaining on three of the four sides. It was quite a distance up.

"We could have been like the Swiss Family Robinson," Amy said. "You know, the ones who were shipwrecked and built a tree house on an island."

"But they got attacked by pirates," Will pointed out.

"Well, we have the men," Amy said.

"I guess so, but why would we need to defend ourselves from them?" Will questioned. "Anyway, let's keep moving."

They resumed walking, but stopped a moment later as they caught sight of some old planks next to some bushes.

Bending down, Joe picked one up. "I wonder what these are doing here?"

"The person who made the tree house probably left them there," Amy said.

Joe nodded. "That's a possibility. They probably brought some planks to the island and these are the ones that were left over."

They continued walking. Apart from a few rabbits and birds, they didn't encounter anything of interest before arriving back at the inlet into which they had sailed into on the Lazy Lucy.

Stopping for a rest, the children sat down on the cliff. They had only been there for about two minutes when they caught sight of a craft as it came into view from around the rocks on the side closest to the mainland.

Sarah stood up. "Hey, what's that?"

Will, who was now carrying the binoculars, peered through them. "It's a rowboat. I can see one person in it."

Joe frowned. "Why would a person come to this island alone?"

"Perhaps he's connected with the men," Amy suggested.

"I say we keep out of sight until we know the answer," Will said.

As the others agreed, all four of them moved back a bit into the bushes and lay down on their stomachs. Gazing out towards the boat, they waited for it to come ashore.

"I wonder if he knows the way through the rocks," Amy said.

"We'll soon see," Joe stated. "If he does, I reckon he's been to this island before."

"He could be like us," Will said.

"Yes, but to do what we did with just one person is a bit trickier, though it is a smaller boat. I guess we'll just have to wait and see," Joe said.

The craft had no trouble making it through the rocks and was soon beached on the sand. The person climbed out and gazed around.

Peering through the binoculars, Amy saw with surprise that it wasn't a man but a youngish looking woman. After grabbing a rucksack from the rowboat, she walked up the path.

Studying her more closely, Amy saw she was wearing khaki shorts and t-shirt. A pair of binoculars hung around her neck. "Do we follow her?"

"Yes," Joe replied. "We need to see if she's a tourist or a crook."

"She doesn't look like a crook," Sarah said.

Amy nodded. "I agree, but I guess we had better be sure."

The four children waited until she had passed them and was far enough in front before they followed her. She headed straight for the hill and, as she walked past the stream and into some trees, the children lost sight of her.

Will, who was in the lead, raced forward. As he came to the stream and looked around, he frowned. "She's disappeared."

"But she was right here," Amy said. "She must have walked faster."

Following Amy, the others raced up the slope. As they arrived at the top, they all looked around. The mysterious woman couldn't be seen.

"Where did she go?" Joe grabbed the binoculars from Will and peered through them as he scanned the surrounding area. No movement could be seen.

Suddenly, they all heard a noise behind them. Turning around, Joe saw the woman standing at the base of an oak tree.

She walked up to them. "Playing cowboys and

Indians are we?" she said in an amused voice.

Amy frowned. "What?"

The woman smiled, her bright blue eyes shining as looked at each of them in turn. "You were following me."

"We weren't," Will lied. "We—"

"Have you by any chance seen three men about?" the woman interrupted.

"Maybe," Joe replied. "Why do you ask?"

The woman reached into her pocket and took out a badge which she held out for the others to see. It was official looking, just like a police officer would have. There was a name on it. It read: Nancy Allen.

The woman smiled. "I'm Detective Allen and, as you might have guessed, I'm a police officer. I'm trying to find three men—"

"We've seen three men," Sarah interrupted.

Nancy looked at her. "Really? Here, on this island?"

Sarah nodded. "They say they are birdwatchers, but they're bad people."

"Really?" Nancy turned to Joe. "Is that true?"

Joe explained how they had met the men earlier. Once he had done so, he looked curiously at the woman. "Why did you come here?"

"I heard a rumour that the men were here," Nancy said. "Now, would you be able to describe the men so I can see if they are the three that I'm trying to find?" As Will did so, the woman nodded. "Yes, it's them. Do you know where they are staying?"

"There's a cabin in the woods on the far side of the island," Amy replied.

"Okay," Nancy said. "Well, I'm trying to find something that the men have stolen, so—"

"What?" Sarah interrupted.

The woman hesitated. "I'm not sure if I should tell

you."

"We'll keep it a secret," Joe said.

"Well, okay," Nancy said. "The men are wanted for stealing paintings from museums. Do you have any idea of where they could be?"

Joe shook his head. "We haven't seen much. We assumed they were not up to any good, but I didn't realise that they had stolen paintings."

"It's very important that they be found, so can you help me locate them?" Nancy asked.

"Why don't you arrest them now?" Will questioned.

"I need the paintings as proof, so I want to make sure that they are with the men before I arrest them." The woman gazed around for a moment before looking at her watch. "It's such a big island, so I need your help. The paintings have to be somewhere close by. Once I find them, I can contact headquarters."

"Golly, another mystery," Amy said.

The woman frowned. "Another mystery? What do you mean?"

Amy smiled. "We, seem to have a habit of attracting mysteries. This will be our fourth one this summer."

"Did you solve the rest of them?" Nancy asked.

Joe nodded. "Yes."

"Well, it's a good thing that I stumbled onto you lot." Nancy smiled. "So, who can help me solve the mystery of the missing paintings?"

Will looked at the others. "I'm sure everyone will agree with me when I say that we will do all we can to put those men in jail."

"Good," Nancy said. "Now, any ideas of where the paintings could be?"

"There's a cabin that the men use in the woods," Sarah piped up. "We haven't searched it though."

"That sounds like a good spot." The woman pointed

towards the church. "What's down there?"

"Oh, nothing much," Joe said. "It's a ruin, so I don't think the paintings would be in there. There are some caves though, but we explored all of them and couldn't find anything."

"There's also a lighthouse, but it was high tide so we couldn't get across and see what it was like," Will said.

Nancy nodded. "The one that sounds the most promising is the cabin. Do you want to lead the way?"

"Okay, but we'll have to keep watch for the men." Will headed down the hill. There was no sign of the men as the group walked past a group of oak trees and neared the church, but as they came in sight of the inlet, Will held up his hand. "I think I hear something."

The group stopped and listened. Angry voices came from the direction of the woods. As they huddled behind two bushes, they spotted the men emerge from the trees. They were talking loudly, but not loud enough to hear the exact words.

However, it was clear that two of the three men were not happy. They walked onto the beach and disappeared from view a minute later as they went behind the cliff.

Will was tempted to follow them to see where they were going, but he knew that this was the perfect time to explore the cabin. He looked at the woman. "The cabin is in the middle of those woods."

"What are we waiting for then?" Nancy asked.

The children knew that the men could return at any minute, so they raced to the woods and hurriedly waked passed the trees and bushes until they reached the building.

The woman went to the door and swung it open. Before she went inside, she turned to the children. "Keep an eye out for the men while I search."

She then disappeared inside the cabin. The children wanted to peep into the building, but instead they obeyed her instructions and kept watch. Three minutes ticked by and still she didn't come out.

Joe turned to Amy who was nearest to him. "I'm going to see what she's up to." He moved off and was just reaching to open the door when it opened and the woman appeared. "What took you so long?"

"It takes time to examine everything without making a mess," Nancy replied. "I couldn't have the men suspect that someone had been through their stuff."

Suddenly, one of the men yelled out. Joe turned to Nancy. "We need to go!" He turned and raced back to Amy.

CHAPTER 9

THE PLAN

As Joe reached Amy, he followed her gaze and saw Will and Sarah running towards them. Behind them, they saw the thin fellow with beady eyes. As soon as the others reached them, the group raced down the path. As the man pursued them, Joe saw that he was gaining ground.

"We have to split up!" Joe yelled. "Let's meet back at the campsite." He turned to the woman. "Follow me." Up ahead, as the path veered left, he went right, followed by Nancy and Sarah, leaving Will and Amy to head left.

As Will and Amy arrived at the campsite, they saw that the others were already there.

"Did the man chase you?" Will asked.

Joe nodded. "Yes, but we were able to lose him. You should have been there. It—"

"Look!" Sarah interrupted as she suddenly spotted a boat.

The others stared across the water, watching as the boat cruised past the island. "What type of boat is it?" Amy asked.

Putting the binoculars to his eyes, Joe peered towards the craft. His face broke into a smile. "It's a police boat!"

"Let's wave like mad," Amy exclaimed. "If the police—"

"No!" the woman interrupted.

"What?" Will said, surprised. "But they can help round up the men."

Nancy shook her head. "Headquarters believe that a local police officer is involved in the thefts."

"Why do they think that?" Joe asked.

"I can't go into the details," Nancy said. "Just trust me. Besides, what we really need is to discover where the paintings are. Once we know that, I'll contact headquarters, and they'll send along plenty of men."

The children fell silent as the boat passed by. Will looked at Nancy. "Can we go back with you?"

Nancy frowned. "Why?"

"Our boat got damaged on some rocks, and I'm not sure if it will get us to the mainland," Will replied.

The woman hesitated, then nodded. "Fine. Now, does anyone have any idea where else we can search?"

"We could search the church and storehouse," Joe replied.

The group moved off, heading towards the ruined buildings. Arriving at the church, Joe was the last one to enter the building and, as he did so, he thought he caught sight of something out of the corner of his eye.

Turning around, he spotted Luke, the man with the ponytail, heading in their direction. He rushed over to the others. "One of the men is coming this way!"

Everyone stopped what they were doing as they peered out of the doorway.

"Do you think he saw us?" Nancy said.

"I don't know, but if we stand here for much longer

he will." Joe leaned against the wall. "We need to hide."

Nancy shook her head. "I need to find those paintings now. So, instead of us running all over the island, why don't we ask him?"

Will looked at the woman. "What? Why would he tell us anything."

Nancy reached into her pocket and pulled out a pistol. "This can be a very persuasive tool if you use it right."

Joe stared at the gun. "Why are you carrying that?"

"I'm a police officer, remember?" Nancy said. "Don't worry, it isn't as though I'm going to shoot him. I just want to find out about the paintings."

"What do you suggest we do?" Amy asked.

"If you can make some noises, he'll come and investigate, and I'll use the weapon as motivation for him to tell us," Nancy said.

"I can make a noise like a cat," Sarah suggested.

Nancy nodded. "That should do it. If only we could trip him up as well." She glanced around, trying to spot something that would do the job. But there was nothing.

"We'll have to trip him up using our legs," Joe said.

"Let's get into position then." Nancy and Will stood by the door while the girls hid below the window. Joe kept his eye on the man from another window. As Luke walked closer, the girls started their performance.

"Meow," Amy said.

"Meow, meow," Sarah said.

Joe saw Luke stop and stare in the direction of the storehouse. He then walked on, but stopped once more as the girls continued to make cat noises. Frowning, he turned and walked towards the storehouse. Joe motioned to the others that the man was coming and everyone fell silent.

The footsteps got louder as the man approached. He stepped through the open door and glanced around. His eyes caught sight of the girls and his facial expression turned from one of amazement to one of anger. He strode towards them.

Luke didn't see the foot that tripped him and he fell to the ground. But he did see the pistol that was pointed at him as he attempted to get up. This was evident by the way he raised his hands straight away. "Don't shoot!"

"On your feet now!" Nancy ordered.

As the man stood up, a thin smile flickered across his face. "Long time no see, Julie."

Will frowned and glanced at Nancy. "Do you know this man?"

Nancy shook her head. "Never seen him in my life."

Luke spat on the ground as he heard Nancy's response. "You haven't changed, have you, Julie?"

"Where are the paintings?" Nancy asked.

"If you help us, the police will go easier on you," Will stated.

"What do the police have to do with this?" Luke sneered.

"Everything," Will replied. "We're going to take the paintings to the police with Nancy's help."

Luke frowned. "Nancy? Who's she?"

Will pointed to the woman. "She's Nancy."

Luke laughed. "If she promised you—"

"Where are the paintings?" Nancy interrupted.

The man hesitated and then pointed. "Up there."

Nancy looked up at the roof. "In the attic?"

"Yes, but you'll never get away with this, Julie," Luke said.

"Stop calling me Julie!" Nancy yelled. "And put your hands behind your back."

As Luke did what he was told, Nancy reached into her rucksack and pulled out some rope. She tied it around his wrists. "Now, how do you get up to the attic?"

"There's a rope ladder in the back corner, right side," Luke said. As Nancy hurried to the spot, he turned to the children. "She was part of our gang."

"What?" Joe exclaimed, stunned.

"Julie split with us a year ago after grabbing the money that we had stolen in a bank heist. If…" Luke paused as Nancy came back with the rope.

"How do I get the rope up there?" Nancy asked.

"Throw it over the two nails that are in the planks just above where you found the rope," Luke replied.

Nancy turned to the children. "Why don't one of you stay here to guard our prisoner while the rest help me search?"

"I'll stay," Joe offered. He sat down as the others followed Nancy.

After Nancy threw the rope over the nails, she started to climb up. Will went next, then the girls.

As Will stepped on the wooden planks, they creaked. "Be careful," he called out. "These have been here for a long time and might give way at any time."

"Looks like some already have," Amy pointed out as she looked across the floor at the gaping holes.

Nancy glanced around, trying to spot anything that looked like a good place to hide paintings. She spotted an old chest up against the far window. "That has to have the paintings in it."

"I guess so." Will looked around. Nothing else could be seen. "We'll have to be careful, though. One wrong step and we could fall right down."

Nancy looked towards Sarah. "Why don't you go first?"

"What?" Amy exclaimed, turning towards the woman. "You're not afraid, are you?"

Nancy laughed. "Of course not. But she is the smallest and lightest person here, so even if she did step on a rotten plank, she should have the best chance of surviving."

"Should?" Amy repeated.

"Well, there's no guarantee—" Nancy said.

"If you want the paintings, go and get them yourself," Amy interrupted as she clutched her sister protectively. "My sister isn't going to risk her life for some paintings."

Sarah looked at Amy. "I'm not scared."

Amy smiled as she raked her hand through her sister's blonde hair. "I know you're not scared. I just don't want you to take a risk for nothing."

"For nothing?" Nancy shouted. "Do you want to put these men in jail or not? If—"

"Shouting isn't going to do you any good," Will interrupted.

"I'm sorry," Nancy said. "I didn't mean to shout. I just want those paintings."

"I think I've got a better idea," Will said.

"You do?" Nancy said, a smile appearing on her face.

Will nodded as he went over to the rope ladder and pulled it up. "If Sarah takes hold of one end of this, we can hold the other. That way, if the plank does give way and she does fall, we can pull her back up."

Nancy smiled. "A great idea." She turned to Sarah. "Will you do it?"

Sarah nodded and she took the end of the ladder. She then took a deep breath and stepped onto the first plank. Silence. She stepped onto the next one. Silence.

The others waited with bated breath as Sarah slowly

but surely got farther and farther away from them. As she did so, Will realised that, while the rope ladder was long, it would only go three quarters of the way. He shuddered to think what could happen in the final section. But he didn't say anything. He just kept his eyes glued on Sarah's feet.

Suddenly, one of the planks creaked loudly. Sarah paused, but nothing happened. She moved onto the next one which also creaked. It creaked louder than the previous one and, before the others knew what was happening, the plank, along with the next one, broke in half!

Frightened, Sarah cried out as she fell down the hole. "Help!"

CHAPTER 10

RUN!

Luckily, Sarah didn't lose her grip on the rope ladder, which meant that instead of hitting the ground she was left dangling a foot below the hole.

Clinging tightly to the rope, Amy called out. "Are you alright, Sarah?"

"I'm fine, just pull me up," Sarah shouted back.

Amy looked at the others. "We pull on three. One, two, three!"

With everyone pulling as hard as they could, Sarah was slowly lifted up through the hole. Once she was out, everyone kept on pulling as they tried to drag her back to them. Suddenly, Sarah yelled out. "Stop!"

Will frowned. "Why?"

Sarah gingerly stood up. "I'm going to continue on."

"No, it's too dangerous," Amy said. "We'll try another way."

"There isn't any other way," Sarah shouted back.

"But you could have been seriously injured!" Will exclaimed.

"Just give me another chance," Sarah protested. "I know I can do it."

"Let her," Nancy said. "It's the only way."

"But she's my sister!" Amy yelled. "I should be the

one doing that."

"She's more than halfway there," Nancy said. "Let her continue."

Amy looked at her sister. "Be extra careful this time, okay?"

Sarah nodded. The others watched as she stood there, trying to decide which way to go. She then moved, taking one step at a time. Soon, she had reached the end of the rope. Before the others could decide what to do, she suddenly dropped the rope and ran the rest of the way to the chest.

Two of the planks broke, but fortunately Sarah was a step ahead and she didn't fall. The others breathed a sigh of relief as the girl reached the chest. "I'll open it and see if the paintings are in here."

The others waited in anticipation as Sarah opened up the lid and shuffled around in the chest.

"What can you see?" Amy asked.

Sarah pulled out something and showed it to the others. It was a white sheet.

Nancy frowned. "Is that all? No paintings?"

Sarah nodded. "A few odds and ends, but yes, that's all."

Nancy frowned as she gazed at the white sheet. "Why would that be in the chest?"

Will grinned. "Of course! I thought it came from up here."

"What are you talking about?" Nancy asked.

"One of the men tried to scare us," Will replied. "Tried to make us believe in ghosts so we would leave the island. I'm pretty sure they would used that sheet when they tried to frighten us."

Nancy laughed. "That's just like them."

"How do you know what these men are like?" Will said, puzzled.

Nancy hesitated. "Oh, I was just meaning that it sounds typical based on what I have read about these men."

Will called out to Sarah. "Is there anything else in there?"

Sarah closed the lid. "No."

Nancy glared down at Luke as she spotted him through the rotten planks. "He lied."

"Well, it probably wasn't the first time he did that," Amy said.

"No, but it'll be his last." Nancy turned to Sarah. "Grab the rope."

Sarah stepped forward. The return wasn't as difficult as before since she knew where to stand, and she was soon back with the others.

After taking the rope ladder, Nancy threw it down the side. Once in place, she climbed down. She strode over to Luke and slapped him on the face. "You lied."

Luke smirked. "Took you long enough to discover that."

Nancy paced back and forth as the others climbed down the rope and joined her. "You will tell me where the paintings are now."

Luke sneered. "Or else what? Are you going to slap me again?"

Nancy laughed as she pulled out her pistol from where it had been tucked next to her waist. "I have more persuasive methods."

"Oh, no!" Will exclaimed.

Nancy glanced at the red haired boy who was standing by the window. "What's up?"

"The others, they're coming here," Will muttered.

Nancy strode to the window and looked out. Marvin and Kenneth were roughly one hundred feet away and closing. "They can't know we're here. When they pass by—"

Luke suddenly cried out. "Help!"

"Why, you…" Nancy hurried over to the man and aimed her weapon at him. "Don't force me to use this." She looked at Joe. "Is there a back exit?"

"I don't know," Joe admitted.

Nancy hurried to the window and fired her pistol. The bullet whistled above the men's heads and they tumbled to the ground before crawling to the nearest bush.

"What did you do that for?" Will asked. "We could have had a chance to slip by them, but now they know for certain we're here."

"Now that they know we're armed, they'll think twice before entering," Nancy snapped. "Besides, I'm not being captured by those men."

"Why?" Joe questioned. "Because they know you?"

Nancy hesitated. "Okay, if you must know, I was one of them."

Joe glanced at Jake. "So you were telling the truth."

Nancy shook her head. "Only half the truth. I stole the bank money, but only after I heard that they were planning to get rid of me."

"So you're not a police officer?" Sarah asked.

Nancy shook her head. "No, but my father was."

As she hurried away to look for a way out, the children crouched together as they decided what to do. "We can't stay here," Will stated.

"But we can't go with her," Amy argued.

"She's not a threat to us. She wants the paintings, not us." Joe smiled as Nancy crashed through the back door. "Hey! she found a way out."

Will stood up. "If we hurry, we can disappear before the men know we're gone." He raced towards the door.

Letting the girls race by him, Joe glanced back

and saw the men near the entrance. As soon as they stepped through, they would see him. He raced after his sisters, hoping he could get through the door before they saw him.

A yell went out just he went through the back door and he knew he had been spotted.

~

By the time the children arrived at the inlet, Nancy was rowing away.

Joe sighed. "I suppose if she was lying about being a police officer, than we should have realised she would be lying about taking us with her."

"We should get back to the campsite before the men find us," Will said. "Now that they know that we're still on the island, they'll be after us."

The children set off for the campsite. As they neared the woods, Joe came to a halt as he saw the three men running towards them. "Blow!"

"Let's hide in the woods," Amy suggested.

"No. We can't let the men find our campsite. We have to lead them away from that area." Will turned towards the hill. "Let's go to the tree house."

"Good idea." Joe sprinted towards the hill. As he reached it, he glanced back and saw that the men were not far behind. He realised they would have a better chance of getting to the tree house if they split up. This would also mean that if the men caught up with them, not all of them would be captured.

So, as they neared the top of the hill, Joe glanced at the others. "We need to split up."

Amy only took a moment to decide. "I'll go with Sarah. If you boys go alone, we'll only have one man each on our tail."

"Are you sure?" Joe asked.

"We'll be fine," Amy said. "Come on, Sarah." The girls headed straight down the slope while Will went left and Joe went right.

For some reason, the section of the hill that the girls were hurrying down had the most number of gorse bushes. And, because of their prickles, it made it necessary for the girls to slow down.

They hadn't actually gone this way before, and Amy was wishing she had chosen a different way. But there was nothing she could do about it now.

"Stop for a minute, I want to see if there's anyone chasing us," Amy whispered. She could hear twigs breaking to the left and right of her, but none behind her. Maybe there wasn't anyone behind them. But what had happened to the third man then?

"What do we do?" Sarah asked.

Amy was just about to answer when she heard twigs breaking as someone crashed through the bushes. "Run!" She turned and pushed through the bushes, not bothering whether or not she got scratched.

Hurrying down the slope, she was surprised to see the bushes suddenly disappear and found herself staring down a steep bed of grass that, eventually, turned into rocks.

Stopping, she was wondering what to do when Sarah bumped into her. The two girls fell and tumbled down the hillside, rolling over and over, going faster with every passing second.

~

Will wasn't afraid of getting lost as he knew where to hide. The last time they had walked past here, he had spotted an old tree with a hollow trunk.

He headed for the tree and hid inside. Careful to be as quiet as possible, he stood as still as a mouse. He heard the pounding of footsteps as his pursuer raced past.

As soon as the footsteps had faded away, Will emerged from the tree trunk and looked around to make sure no one had spotted him. Satisfied that no one had, he headed towards the tree house.

~

Joe was wishing he had stayed on the path that he had been on. It would have led him to the tree house. But, with the man right behind him, or so it had seemed, he had turned right, hoping to lose him in the trees.

However, as he raced forward, he found himself out in the open. The sandy beach was in front of him and, apart from the woods that he had just come from, he couldn't see anywhere to hide. Hearing someone closing in on him, Joe raced along the sand. Seeing some rocks up ahead, an idea came into his head.

He passed two rocks before he dropped down and hid behind the third one. His feet were partly sticking out, so he shuffled some sand over them. He lay still as he heard the man approach. The next minute or two would tell whether or not he would be caught.

CHAPTER 11

THE QUARRY

Amy and Sarah came to a stop at the bottom of the hillside. After sitting up in a daze, the girls looked around and discovered they were next to a quarry. Hidden by trees and bushes on all sides, there were piles of rocks strewn all over the area. There also seemed to be a hole, which indicated to Amy that it might also be a mine.

"Golly, how come we didn't see this before?" Amy asked.

"What is it?" Sarah said.

"It must be where they got the rocks from to build the church and other buildings on this island. After all, it would have been a bit difficult to transport all that rock from the mainland." Amy stood up and walked around, forgetting for a minute that someone was chasing them.

Hearing a noise, she glanced up and saw Marvin as he emerged from the bushes. He hurried down the hill.

Realizing that they had to hide somewhere, she hurried over to the hole. As soon as she saw that there was a ladder, she started climbing down it, her sister right behind her.

The ladder was old, but still in good condition. Once she was on solid ground, she switched on the torch that she had been carrying in her pocket and swung it around. There were at least four tunnels going in opposite directions. She didn't know which one to go down, but as she heard the man's footsteps, she chose the one closest to her.

The light bobbed to and fro as Amy and Sarah hurried down the tunnel. The light from the torch picked up the wooden supports, and Amy hoped that they weren't going to give out while they were nearby.

After they had walked for some distance, Amy slowed down and looked at her sister. "Are you alright?"

Sarah nodded. "I can't hear the man behind us, so hopefully he didn't see us go down the hole."

Amy listened and realised that her sister was right. No sound could be heard. She switched off the torch. "We'll wait here and see if we hear anything."

~

At the tree house, Will was waiting for Joe and the girls to arrive. He swung his legs back and forth as he sat on the platform and gazed down, searching through the leaves for any sign of movement. But none could be seen.

A minute later, he caught sight of someone heading towards him. He held his breath as he waited to see who it was. A moment later, he saw it was Joe.

Joe started climbing up. As he reached the halfway point, he called up. "Are the girls with you?"

Will shook his head. "No."

Joe frowned and resumed climbing, reaching the top a minute later. As he reached the platform and sat down, he turned to Will. "How long have you been here?"

"About ten minutes," Will replied. "I was just starting to wonder if everyone else had been captured when I saw you through the trees."

"It took longer than I thought to get rid of the man following me," Joe admitted. "I had to hide behind some rocks and wait until he passed until I could head for here."

"I hope the girls are safe," Will said. "We'll give them thirty minutes. If they don't show up by then, we'll start searching."

Joe nodded. "If they don't come back in that time, I'm afraid something may have happened to them."

~

After waiting for what seemed like forever, Amy switched the torch back on. "I haven't heard anything for a while, so we could head back."

"Okay," Sarah replied.

Amy led the way back. She wasn't concerned about getting lost since this tunnel only split into two and the second tunnel was much smaller than the first.

The girls were nearly at the end of the tunnel when Amy heard a noise. She stopped, causing Sarah to bump into her. "What's wrong?"

"I thought I heard something," Amy whispered as she switched off her torch. "Wait here." She continued along the tunnel until she came to the bend which was quite close to the shaft.

Peering around, she saw a shadow in the darkness. She wondered what it could be when a cough broke the silence. It was one of the men!

Amy turned and tiptoed back, wondering how long

they would have to stay in the mine.

~

With heavy hearts, the boys climbed down from the tree. Once on solid ground, they discussed what to do.

"We should go to the top of the hill and see if we can see anything," Joe suggested.

Will led the way up the hill. Once they had reached the top, he looked around. No one could be seen. "What do we do now?"

"Go the way the girls went." Joe took the lead and hurried down the hill. He soon encountered the prickly bushes that had slowed down the girls and, while this wasn't good for the arms and legs, it did prove something as he caught sight of something blue.

It was a small piece of fabric. Joe turned to Will. "This looks as though it's come from Sarah's shorts."

Will nodded. "So now we know that they made it this far." He continued on, stopping when they came into sight of the quarry. "Gosh, I didn't know this was here."

Joe shook his head. "Nor me. We must have missed it because of all those tall bushes." A thought struck him as he caught sight of a shaft going into the ground. "You don't suppose the girls are underground, do you?"

"It's a possibility." Will suddenly clutched hold of Joe and pulled him down to the ground.

"What—" Joe said.

"Quiet!" Will pointed to the shaft as one of the men emerged from it. As he saw his bald head, he realised it was Marvin.

As the man looked around, the boys ducked behind a clump of bushes. They froze, wondering if they had been seen.

Apparently satisfied that no one was about, Marvin sat down on a nearby rock.

The boys waited for a minute or two, but the man didn't move. Creeping back a tad, Will whispered to Joe. "There's only one reason why he would sit there."

"If he was waiting for someone to come out of the shaft," Joe said.

Will nodded. "And I don't think he's waiting for his friends."

"No, so it looks as though the girls are down there," Joe said.

"What do we do about it?" Will asked.

Joe thought for a moment before he answered. "We have to distract the man."

"What if we throw a rock into the other end of the quarry?" Will suggested. "While he sees what the noise is, we can slip into the hole."

Joe grinned. "Good thinking." He searched the ground for a rock that would be suitable for the diversion. It needed to be small enough to go a long distance, but big enough to make a loud noise when it landed. He found one a few seconds later. "This should do it."

Will parted the bushes with his hand. Looking down at the man, he calculated where the rock needed to land. After pointing this out to Joe, he waited for him to throw it.

The rock sailed out of Joe's hand a second later. As it fell towards the ground, he hoped it would hit the pile of rocks that were past the two small bushes. That would provide some cover for them when they raced down.

Unfortunately, it didn't get that far. As it landed five feet short of the bushes, Joe grimaced. Still hoping for the best, he waited at the edge of the bushes.

As soon as the rock hit the other rocks, the man stood up, frowned, and walked over to the bushes.

Joe and Will raced down the hill. After reaching the rocky ground, they spurted towards the hole. But, before they could get there, the man turned around and headed back.

The boys ducked behind a rock, certain they had been seen. Luckily, at that very moment, there was a yell as someone called out. Peeking out from behind the rock, Joe saw Luke walk towards the quarry.

"I lost sight of my kid," Luke called. "What about yours?"

"They went down the tin mine," Marvin replied.

The boys heard his footsteps retreat and they breathed a sigh of relief. They didn't know what Marvin had seen that interested him enough to walk towards them, but it had obviously been nothing since he was now engaged in a conversation with the other man.

With the wind in the other direction, the boys could only hear scraps of the conversation between them. Words like food, torch, and rope.

As the talking subsided, Joe peeked around the rock and saw Marvin leaving the quarry. Looking in the opposite direction, he saw Luke sitting in the same spot as Marvin had been sitting.

Joe turned to Will. "We have to do something before Marvin gets back. We can't do anything if they're both here, but we might be able to outsmart one of them."

"What about throwing a rock?" Will suggested.

"But we tried that and it didn't work," Joe replied.

"We're closer now," Will said. "If we threw it from here, it would have to go past those bushes. I'm sure it would give us enough time to go down the shaft."

Since Joe was unable to come up with a better plan, he decided to give it one more attempt. After finding a rock, Will took aim and hurled it. As soon as Luke moved, so did they.

Reaching the shaft first, Joe climbed down. Will glanced over at Luke before he climbed down and was relieved to see that he was still behind the bushes. He breathed a sigh of relief as he followed his friend down into the darkness.

Joe switched on his torch and shone it around. The girls were nowhere in sight.

After deciding to go down the nearest tunnel, the boys walked along it, calling as they went. They hadn't gone far before a light was shone upon them.

It was the girls. They hugged the boys, relieved that help had arrived.

"How did you find us?" Sarah asked.

"When you didn't show up at the tree house, Will and I went searching," Joe said. "When we saw a man sitting near the quarry shaft, we put two and two together."

"Is the man still waiting?" Amy asked.

"Yes, but I've thought of a way to get out," Joe replied.

CHAPTER 12

THE RAFT

Five minutes later, Sarah poked her head through the top of the shaft and called out to Luke, startling him. "Help! My sister's in trouble."

Luke hurried over. "Show me the way."

The two climbed down the shaft, stopping when they reached the bottom. Sarah turned to Luke. "She's this way."

Sarah walked quickly down a tunnel and, as she heard Luke following behind, she grinned. She counted the corners to herself as she went around them. "One, two, three."

A few seconds passed and then she heard Luke cry out. She turned around as he fell down, landing on the dirt.

A second later, the boys appeared with Amy. "Come on!" They turned and raced back up the tunnel with Sarah following close behind.

Upon reaching the ladder, the girls went up first, and then Will. Joe glanced back down the tunnel and was glad that the man couldn't be seen. Without a torch, he would be much slower than them and, Joe hoped, that would give them enough time to get to the campsite unseen.

~

Arriving back at the campsite, Will looked towards the cave. "We need to see if there's any way to get the Lazy Lucy to sail again. The men will start searching this island from top to bottom soon, and it would be best if we're away by then. But there's no need for everyone to get their feet wet."

Will turned towards the girls. "If you could pack up the tent and everything else, that would be helpful."

Amy nodded. "Will do." As she and Sarah went to work, the boys took off their shoes and socks and waded into the water.

They went into the cave and approached the boat. It had more water in it than before since it wasn't low tide, and Will frowned as he climbed over the side and walked around. "I was thinking that we might have been able to bail out the water as we sailed along, but even with all four of us doing that, I'm not sure if that would work."

"Well, in order for us to try that, we'd have to get it out of this cave first," Joe said.

"What's the problem with that?" Will asked.

"Well, the only reason that the Lazy Lucy isn't sinking now is that it's in shallow water," Joe replied. "As soon as we move it out of the cave, it will be in deeper water."

"So we'll have to do it at low tide exactly," Will said. "And we'll only get one chance at it."

"Yes." Joe waded out of the cave as he continued talking. "We still have another two hours or so until low tide, so hopefully we can hide till then."

The boys dried themselves and joined the girls in eating tinned fruit. They told the girls what they had discussed and, afterwards, the girls told them that they had packed up everything except one tent that they couldn't get down.

After Will finished eating, he went over to the tent. With Joe's help, he started taking it apart while the girls washed the dishes in the nearby water.

Suddenly, they heard voices coming towards them. Amy dropped the dishes and hurried along the sand until she came to a bend. She took one glance around the rocks before she turned and raced back, shouting as she went.

"The men," Amy yelled. "They're coming this way!"

"They must be searching for our boat," Will muttered. "That's why they're going along the shore."

"What shall we do?" Sarah asked.

"Grab whatever you can and head inside the woods." Will grabbed hold of the tent and the rucksack and headed towards the trees.

The others quickly grabbed some tins of food, the matches, the torches, sleeping bags, and a few other odds and ends. They had just reached the cover of the trees when the men came into view.

As the men came to a stop, Will realised that they had probably spotted the footprints in the sand and, as they bent down, knew that he was right.

Within moments, the men had found the fireplace along with the tent and the other stuff that the children hadn't had time to grab.

They talked amongst themselves for a matter of minutes as the children watched from the shelter of the bushes but, since the wind was blowing in the opposite direction, they couldn't hear anything.

The men headed back onto the sand and the fellow with the ponytail waded into the water as he went into the cave. He shouted and re-appeared a moment later, smiling.

The children crawled through the bushes until they could see the entrance of the cave and, as they watched, the three men disappeared inside it.

"What do you think they're going to do?" Amy asked.

"Smash the boat," Will muttered angrily.

A minute later, the Lazy Lucy appeared as the men pulled it out of the cave. The men grabbed the oars, broke them in half, and hurled them into the water. Then, they dragged the boat deeper into the water.

"That's the end of her," Joe said in disappointment as he saw the boat fill with water.

Within a matter of seconds, the boat was half full of water and, less than a minute later, it disappeared underneath the swirling water. The men smiled and laughed as they walked back to the campsite.

Motioning for the others to follow him, Will took the tent and rucksack and headed deeper into the trees. Once he was far enough away, he looked at the others. "Those men will stay there until we return, so that's the end of that campsite."

"And the end of the Lazy Lucy," Amy said. "I know it was just a boat, but after we spent all that time fixing her up—"

"And painting her," Sarah interrupted.

"It was sad to see her disappear," Amy said. "I don't suppose we could get her back up when low tide comes?"

Will shook his head. "She's too deep. Even at low tide, we couldn't raise her off the sand. No, I'm afraid we'll have to find another way to get off this island."

"Why don't we search for the boat that the men use?" Sarah suggested.

"Well, we didn't see it when we searched the island, so I don't see much point in searching again," Will admitted. "No, we need something different."

"Hey, what about that pile of wood that we saw near the tree house?" Joe said.

"What about it?" Amy asked.

"Couldn't we use it to build a raft?" Joe questioned. "We don't have a sail so we would have to row, but even if we paddled with our hands, we could still get to the mainland. It might take a while, but it's worth a try. Every minute longer that we stay on this island, the greater chance we have of being caught by the men. And they'll be sitting at that campsite for some time, so now's the perfect opportunity."

"But that wood is on the other side of the island," Sarah pointed out. "And the mainland is this side."

"I know, but it can't be helped unless we use the branches that are lying around here, but those planks of wood will be a whole lot better than the branches." Joe turned to Will. "What do you think?"

"Let's do it. Let's go now before the men spot us." Will grabbed as much as he could and hurried off.

The others collected what was left and followed Will. They trudged through the woods and, before long, they were at the tree house. After they had dumped their stuff beside some bushes and hid it from view with some branches, they searched for the wooden planks.

With each person carrying what they could, they made their way to the beach. This side of the island was pretty rocky with cliffs on either side, so it probably wasn't the best place to launch the raft, but they could still build it here.

Joe dropped his share of the wood. "We'll need some vines. We have some rope, but not enough."

Will turned to Amy and Sarah. "Why don't you girls search for some vines?" As the girls raced off, he looked at Joe. "We should find some sturdy branches. This wood won't be enough for the entire raft, so we'll need some pieces that are the same size as these planks. Let's get them first."

The boys hurried away. By the time they arrived back, they saw that the girls had already found some vines and had gone to get more.

Getting to work on the raft, the boys tied the planks together using the rope. They wanted the middle to be the sturdiest, so the vines would be left to last.

From time to time they stopped when they heard noises in the nearby bushes, but it either turned out to be the girls or an animal.

Finally, Will pulled tight the last vine and stood up. The raft was finished. "What do you think of it?"

Sarah studied it. "It looks small."

"As long we can all fit on it I'm happy," Amy stated. "Besides, the mainland isn't too far away."

"What are we going to use as paddles?" Joe asked.

"I left this plank of wood here," Will said, pointing to a small piece. "It was too small for the raft, so I thought that one of us could use it as a paddle."

"It's a pity our oars got broken," Sarah said.

Will nodded. "We could probably dive down and rescue part of one, but I don't think it's worth taking the time or the risk." He glanced at his watch. "It's time to go."

"Are we leaving right now?" Amy asked.

"Yes, the sooner we leave the better. We can carry the raft to…" Will paused as he heard a noise. Looking towards the bushes, he waited.

This time, instead of an animal, a face with beady eyes appeared. It was Kenneth.

CHAPTER 13

WE'RE DROWNING!

As the man yelled out, Will turned to the others. "We have to go now!"

As Kenneth headed towards them, the children took hold of the raft and ran to the water. Luckily, they were quite close. As the raft touched the water, Joe glanced back towards the bushes. The man was now on the rocks and hurrying towards them.

Everyone reacted instantly. After pushing the craft further out into the water, they climbed on. Sarah went first while Will, after giving it one last shove, joined them.

"Hey! Come back here!" Kenneth shouted as he stood at the edge of the water.

The children didn't answer as they used their hands to paddle further out into the water. The waves slammed against the nearby rocks, and it took all their hard work to avoid them. It was slow progress and, just as they passed the rocks, an extra big wave hit them, crashing over the raft. Everyone was soaked.

"Maybe this wasn't such a good idea after all," Amy said as she brushed her long, brown hair away from her eyes.

Joe glanced back towards the beach and saw the

beady-eyed man had been joined by Marvin, the bald man. He turned to the others. "We can't turn back now. If we did, the men would certainly catch us."

"We have to get to the mainland," Will said. "Once there we'll be safe."

As another big wave soaked them, Sarah shivered. "I'm scared."

Amy hugged her. "I'm right here. There's nothing to be afraid of."

"But I'm not as good a swimmer as you are," Sarah replied.

"We aren't sinking yet," Joe said. "But if we do, I'll be right by your side, as will Amy. Okay?"

As Sarah nodded, Joe glanced back at the beach to see how much progress they had made. They had travelled some distance but, unfortunately, they were drifting alongside the coast and not away from it. "As long as we don't go over any..." He paused as he heard a scraping noise. He shouted out. "We've hit a rock!"

Before anyone could reply, the raft broke apart. As it split in half, the children fell into the water, disappearing from view.

Breaking the surface moments later, Joe glanced around. He spotted Will, but none of his sisters. Worried, he took a breath and dived underneath the water. He saw a shape to the left of him. Kicking as fast as he could, he swam over and found that it was Amy. He helped her to the surface. "Where's Sarah?"

Amy whipped her head around, searching for her younger sister. "I don't know."

Joe turned to Will who was holding onto the part of the raft that was still floating. "We have to find Sarah."

Both boys disappeared underneath the waves. Joe didn't see anything at first in the murky water, but then he caught sight of something. Swimming closer, he saw it was Sarah. She was thrashing her arms about.

Kicking his feet, he swam closer and grabbed her. He kicked upwards. As he did so, he felt hands grab him. Together, they shot up to the surface. Within a minute, Joe was feeling like his old self again.

However, it took Sarah a few more minutes before she gave a slight grin. "I wouldn't want to go through that again. I thought I was going to drown. A bit of wood from the raft must have hit me. For a few moments, I felt really strange."

Joe smiled as he gave Sarah's arm a squeeze. "You know I wouldn't let anything happen to you." He looked towards the rocky beach and saw that they had been drifting closer to it. Kenneth was still standing on the rocks, watching them.

"I saw the bald man race off a short while ago," Will said. "If I had to guess, I would say they saw us break apart and rushed to get their boat." He looked along the coast and saw a rowboat appear around the bend of the island.

Amy followed his gaze and saw the craft as well. "We'd better call it quits. We can't go on now that we only have a piece of the raft left."

Will nodded. "Let's head for the shore."

Hanging onto the wood, they kicked towards the beach. As they did so, Joe suddenly saw something. They had been drifting along the side of the island and were now next to some cliffs. "Hey! Why don't we hide in that cave over there."

"Let's just go back," Amy said.

"Don't you want to stop the men?" Joe asked.

"Yes, but not if we—" Amy replied.

"Yes or no?" Joe interrupted.

Amy hesitated. But, as she saw the rowboat getting closer, she nodded. "What do we do?"

"Pretend to drown and then swim to the cave. Will can go first and you girls can follow him to make sure you don't get lost," Joe replied.

"Only if Sarah says yes," Amy said.

Sarah hesitated and looked at her sister. "Okay, but stay close to me."

Will agreed to the plan and, a moment later, yelled out. "Help!"

"We're drowning!" Joe shouted. Out of the corner of his eye, he spotted the bald man in the rowboat react.

Will disappeared under the water, then Sarah, then Amy. Joe yelled out once more before also diving down. Before he knew it, they were inside the cave. Luckily, it wasn't high tide, so only half of the cave was flooded.

As the children relaxed, they could hear the men yell out. Peering through the entrance of the cave, Will saw the man from the rowboat jump into the water. "They're searching for us."

"They can search all they want out there," Joe said as he leaned against the rocks. It wasn't the most comfortable place to rest, but the swimming had tired him out and anything felt good right about now.

The situation stayed the same for the next few minutes, but then it changed as Sarah noticed that the men were coming towards them. "Oh, no! We'll be discovered."

"If we move to the back of the cave, we might be able to find a hiding place," Will said. "But hurry! They're almost here."

After getting to their feet, the children stepped over the rocks as they went deeper into the cave. The cave itself wasn't that large, mostly thin and narrow, so they hadn't gone far before they had to stop.

Leaning against the cave wall, Will listened to the

men talking near the entrance.

"Let's see if they're in the cave," Marvin said.

"But I saw them drown," Kenneth said.

"Then why haven't we seen any bodies?" Marvin asked. "This is the only cave along this part of the shoreline, so let's search it."

"But we don't have any torches," Kenneth argued.

"We'll use our eyes," Marvin said. "It's not going to be too dark."

As the men walked forward, their eyes scanning the walls, Will looked back at the others. "Can you squeeze behind that rock?"

Joe saw the rock that Will meant and investigated. Straight away, he saw that there was a pile of rubble all around it.

Frowning, he glanced up and saw that there seemed to be some sort of hole, and that was where the rock had fallen from. Peering closer, he couldn't see an end to the hole, so he whispered to the others. "Look what I've found."

The others came closer and saw the hole. Will looked back at the men who were now halfway through the cave. They probably had twenty seconds or so before they would be discovered.

"Into the hole," Will whispered. "It's our only chance." He scrambled past Joe and crawled into the hole.

Joe waited for the girls to climb in before he did. Looking back, he saw that the men were almost on him and so, without waiting for Amy to fully disappear from view, he climbed in.

In his haste to hurry, Joe squeezed up against the side of the hole and tried to get even with his sister, but he regretted this as soon as the dirt and rocks started to fall.

The landslide only lasted a few seconds, but it felt like minutes. Scrambling forward, Amy and Joe bumped into the others who had stopped.

Hearing the dirt and rocks fall behind them, Will moved forward a bit more and realised that the tunnel was now wider and taller. "You can stand up over here."

"I can't see," Sarah whimpered.

"I'll put out my hand," Will said.

Soon, they were all standing in the darkness and touching each other. "That rock fall caused us to lose the light," Joe stated.

"We might be able to move the rock fall," Amy said. "After all, it only went for a few seconds." She moved back along the tunnel and had just reached the spot when the roof rumbled and caved in again.

This time, it was louder than before and went on for longer.

CHAPTER 14

A WAY OUT

"Amy!" Joe called out as he scrambled towards the sound. He couldn't see anything so he had to use his hands to feel around. He felt something soft and pulled his sister out of harms way.

"Thanks," Amy said. "That was too close."

The two walked back to the others. "There's no way we can get out that end," Joe said.

"Well, the tunnel seems to keep on going at this end, so let's stop talking and walk," Will suggested. "We don't know how much air we have in this tunnel so the sooner we get out of here the better."

"It's just like the tunnel underneath Bracknesh Castle," Amy said.

"Except this one is bigger." Joe stretched his hands out wide and found that, while it wasn't the width of his arms, it was still quite big. "I'll lead the way. We can hold hands to keep together."

It was slow going as they felt their way along the tunnel. Joe soon realised that this wasn't an ordinary tunnel and, as it widened and got taller, an idea sprung into his mind. "Let's stop for a moment."

"Why?" Amy asked.

"I just thought of where this tunnel could lead," Joe

replied.

"Where?" Will questioned.

"To the quarry," Joe stated.

"Why do you say that?" Amy asked.

"Well, I don't see why smugglers would create this tunnel, and it seems too big and tall for a natural tunnel," Joe replied.

"That does make sense," Will said. "The quarry is quite close by."

"And we didn't explore all the tunnels," Amy said.

"So, now that we think we know where the tunnel leads, what do we do?" Sarah asked.

"Continue," Joe said. "It's all we can do."

With renewed hope, the children resumed walking. They had lost track of time down in the darkness and so, when Joe came to a halt some time later, they didn't know how long they had been walking.

"What's up?" Will asked.

"We've come to another tunnel," Joe replied. "I've been feeling around and I can't touch any rock, so that's why I'm assuming this one has joined with another tunnel."

"Which way do we go?" Sarah questioned.

Will thought about what direction they had been travelling in. "I would say that the mine entrance is closer to the right than the left. So if we have an option to go right, I say we take it."

Joe walked into the middle, or at least where he thought the middle was. Everyone spread out and ascertained where the walls were.

Deciding that they may as well follow Will's suggestion, they headed right. This tunnel seemed much straighter than the other one and this confirmed that they were probably in the mine.

They were all feeling the cold from their wet clothes

and the cold tunnel didn't help. Even Will, who prided himself on being tough, was starting to get really cold. He didn't know how the girls were taking it, but he hoped that they would soon be out of the tunnel and sitting beside a roaring fire. Imagining the fire already, Will continued on.

Suddenly, Joe called out. "I think I see light up ahead."

The others looked over Joe's shoulder and saw a glimmer of light. Eager to see where it was coming from, they hurried forward. The light grew brighter and they saw that it was the entrance to the mine.

They rushed forward, all eager to be the first one out into the sunlight. Reaching an intersection, Joe stopped. "Hey, that's the tunnel we went down."

Will nodded. "Yes. And at the time we wondered where this one went."

"Well, now we know." Joe hurried forward and was soon climbing up the metal ladder. As the others scrambled up after him, he stepped onto the grass. The sun shone down on him, instantly making him feel a whole lot warmer. He lay down on the grass. "Phew, it's good to be out in the open again."

The others joined him as they soaked up the warmth of the sun. "I couldn't agree more," Amy said.

"Especially since our clothes are wet," Sarah pointed out. "I'm never going into that mine again."

"Well, there's no need to go down it again," Will said. "Now that the men think that we've drowned, they won't bother trying to hide what they are up to."

"But first we have to get dry," Amy said. "If I stay in these clothes any longer, I'll feel that they are part of my body."

"What about the smoke?" Joe questioned. "Won't the men see it and wonder where it's coming from?"

"As long as the wood is dry and we don't create too much smoke, we'll be fine." Will looked up at the sun. "I don't know what time it is since my watch was damaged in the water, but it will getting dark soon, so let's get going."

They stood up and walked to the spot where they had camped the first night. After picking up the wood that they had put there the previous night, they made their way to the beach.

The boys soon had a small fire going and they realised that, in order for them to dry their clothes quickly, they would have to make a bigger fire.

"We could wait till the men leave," Joe suggested.

Sarah frowned. "Why would the men leave?"

"If they're thieves, they have to steal from time to time, right?" Joe questioned. "So, they would have to leave this island to do it. They probably sneak away in their boat to the mainland, steal something, and bring it back here. It's almost the perfect setup."

"Almost?" Amy repeated.

Joe nodded. "Yes. They didn't expect us to camp here and put a stop to their plan."

"But we haven't stopped them," Amy argued. "We don't even know much about them."

"But we will." Joe frowned as he saw a bunch of smoke blowing up from the fire. "Hey, who put that damp branch on?" He reached forward and tried to take the branch out but it was already half alight. As there was nothing he could do about it he let it burn, hoping that the men wouldn't spot the smoke.

~

As time passed, the clothes began to get dry. The children, all worn out from their swim in the water and the trek in the tunnel, lay down beside the fire and had soon dozed off to sleep.

Waking up some time later, Joe realised it was quite late. The glow from the setting sun was just visible above the horizon. He estimated that they had half an hour or so before darkness arrived.

He woke the others and, together, decided what to do. While Amy and Sarah went back to get the torches and some tinned food, the boys would stir up the fire. Their clothes were mostly dry, but their shoes were still damp and they didn't want to be walking in shoes that were still wet.

Once the girls arrived back, the children placed all the damp stuff closest to the fire which was roaring once more.

As darkness spread across the island, Joe turned to Will. "We need to have another look in the cabin where the men sleep."

"But that woman didn't find the paintings there," Sarah said.

"I know the paintings won't be there, but it's the best place to start the search," Joe replied.

"But we can only do that if the men leave the island tonight," Amy said. "I know we talked about this before, but they wouldn't leave every night, so why would they go tonight?"

"They might not, but then again, they might," Joe admitted. "They seemed very anxious to get us off the island as soon as possible, so that might mean that someone might be coming to pick up the paintings. And, before that happened, they would probably want to steal another painting."

Will nodded. "That makes sense, but the only way we'll know is if we keep an eye on the inlet near the cabin. If anyone is going to be leaving the island, it will be from that point. But I can't see them leaving for a while, so let's eat some food first."

After a quick meal, they smothered the fire with sand, picked up everything that was lying around, and moved off.

It seemed as though several hours had passed before a bobbing light could be seen, but it could have been more or it could have been less as Joe had no way of knowing. He woke the others who were dozing on the grass above the beach.

They peered through the bushes as they watched the man with a ponytail and glasses walk along the beach and disappear from view.

"I wonder where he's going," Will muttered.

"Hopefully, he's going to get the boat," Joe said. "They must have one hidden somewhere."

Everyone fell silent. Inside five minutes, a moving light could be seen near the woods as though someone was walking towards the beach. Since the wind was blowing in their direction, they were able to hear talking.

"It's two men," Joe said. "Now, if the first one appears with a boat…" He paused as he saw a light in the water. He picked up the binoculars and looked through them.

"What can you see?" Sarah asked.

"It's a rowboat," Joe replied. "It has to be the man who we saw just before. He's just beached the craft and the men are now climbing on board. Now they're pushing off."

Will took the binoculars from Joe and gazed through them. "It will take some time to get to the mainland and back again, not to mention how long it will take to steal a painting, if that's what they're doing."

Joe nodded. "We'll have quite a few hours, but we

don't know how long it will take to find the paintings, and we'll have to move slower in the darkness, so let's get going."

"Hadn't we better wait a few more minutes until the men disappear from sight?" Amy asked. "If they were to see a flash of light, they would head straight back."

"Good thinking." Will looked back towards the mainland and waited for the rowboat to disappear from view.

CHAPTER 15

KEEPING WATCH

As Amy followed Joe into the cabin and looked around, she could see there were just the basics. Some sleeping bags, some tinned food, a lamp, some matches, and a couple of rucksacks.

Joe and Will searched through the rucksacks while the girls went through the other stuff.

"There can't be any paintings here because that woman would have found them," Amy said as she stood up and surveyed the cabin.

"Well, it was worth a try." Joe pulled out a scruffy bird book from one of the rucksacks. "This is probably where they got the information about the Dodo from."

"But what about the paintings?" Sarah said. "There's nothing here."

"I didn't think the paintings would be here," Joe admitted. "However, I did think we might have been able to find something that would give us a clue to where they were."

The children quickly searched the rest of the men's belongings, but it didn't help. Leaving the cabin, Will shone the torch around. "Where shall we search next?"

"There were one or two caves over on the other side of the island that we didn't search before as it was high tide, but now that it is almost low tide, we should be able search them without getting wet," Joe said.

Everyone agreed that this was the best move, so they headed to the caves. It took ten minutes to search the two caves and nothing was found. Disheartened, the children sat on the sand and discussed what to do.

"Well, there's only the lighthouse left," Will said. "If they're not in there, I don't know where they would be. And, with it being low tide, it's the best time to get across." He stood up and walked away.

The others followed him, the lights from the torches bobbing to and fro as they walked.

~

The moon shone brightly as the children arrived at the rocks. Since it was almost a full moon, they could see even without using their torches that the rocks had no water over them. In fact, the water was so low that even some of the sand was visible.

Joe was the first one to step onto the rocks and the others followed him. The rocks probably hadn't had water on them for over an hour so they weren't slippery, but walking across them was still somewhat perilous as they were jagged in places.

When they arrived at the lighthouse, Joe went to the door and twisted the handle. Nothing happened. "I wonder why it's locked."

Sarah's green eyes gleamed. "The paintings must be in there!"

"Not necessarily," Will said. "It could have been locked by whoever last operated it. If they let everyone in there, the place would be damaged in no time."

"I still think the paintings are in there," Sarah said.

"Well, we can't prove it either way." Joe gazed

upwards at the railing that went around the little platform at the top of the lighthouse. "Though, if we could somehow get up there we could get in."

"What about using a rope?" Amy suggested.

Joe shook his head. "You couldn't throw a rope that far up. Besides, it would need to support your weight as you climbed, so it would also need to grip onto something. No, I'm afraid that's out of the question."

Will tried to open the door himself. When that didn't work, he pushed against it. But that didn't work either. The girls shivered as a big wave smashed against the rocks nearby, covering them in a stream of spray.

"Let's move on," Amy said. "There's no use standing here if we can't get in."

"So what do you suggest we do?" Joe asked.

Amy shrugged. "I don't know. But I'm getting tired of walking around."

"Let's head back to the campsite," Will suggested. "I can't think of anywhere else we can search for the paintings, and from there we can keep watch for the men."

"If we follow the men when they return, they might lead us to where they're hiding the paintings," Joe said.

Will smiled. "Exactly."

~

It didn't take as long to set up camp as it had the other night since they only had one tent and half of their belongings.

Joe suggested that Will take the first watch while he and the girls got some sleep. Will was happy to do that, so he took the binoculars and a torch and walked up the hill.

As the girls climbed into the tent, Joe decided to

start a fire to keep warm. After warming his hands, an overwhelming tiredness came over him so he lay down.

After sleeping for a while, Joe was shaken awake by Will. He groggily stood up "Did you see anything?"

"Not a single thing." Will handed the torch and binoculars to Joe and lay down beside the fire.

As Joe climbed up the hill, he was glad that it wasn't too far away, though it still felt like a trek in the middle of the night. Reaching the top, he turned off his torch and sat down. Peering upwards, he saw that the moon had gone behind a cloud.

A cold breeze was blowing across the island and he stood up and paced back and forth to keep warm. He did this for ten minutes and sat down. Peering through the binoculars, he looked towards the inlet. Nothing out of the ordinary could be seen. He had no idea when the men would return. For all he knew, they could be gone for a day or even two days.

He put the binoculars down and thought about everything that had happened in the last two days. It had been an action packed time, but also scary. It wasn't as though he was scared now, but when he had been searching for Sarah in the water, that had been scary. He was glad that they weren't going to build another raft, for the same thing might happen again.

He thought about what his parents would say when they learnt about everything that had happened. They wouldn't be happy but, if the men were caught, they would be proud of them.

He didn't know how long he sat staring up at the stars but, as his eyelids began to close and he got sleepy, he thought that he would head back down the hill. He hurried down and found the fire almost out and Will fast asleep. He put some more wood on the fire and went to wake the girls.

Peering in the tent, he saw his sisters peacefully sleeping and decided that he would take the next shift. They were younger than him and, especially after the swimming drama, Sarah needed all the sleep that she could get. And if he woke Amy, Sarah might also wake.

After walking back to the fire, he decided to lie down and warm up for a few minutes before heading back to his post. He lay down, closed his eyes, and before he knew what hit him, he was fast asleep.

He woke as the first rays of sunshine appeared over the horizon. Stumbling to his feet, he realised he had been asleep for hours. But before he could be annoyed with himself, he heard a noise in the sky.

Looking towards the sound, he spotted a seaplane as it flew over the island. He shook Will awake before calling to the girls who were still sleeping inside the tent.

As the girls scrambled out, Joe looked up at the sky again, but the seaplane had vanished from view. He could still hear it though, so it was somewhere close by.

"What is it?" Amy said.

"A seaplane. If we climb to the top of the hill we might be able to see it land." Joe hurried towards the hill, the others racing after him. Puffing and panting, they arrived at the top of the hill in time to see the seaplane in the inlet as it taxied across the water.

"They must have a big operation," Will stated.

"Why do you say that?" Amy asked.

"Because it would cost a ton of money to buy that machine, not counting the petrol that they would use—" Will said.

"But aren't some paintings worth a lot of money?" Sarah interrupted.

"Yes, but what I'm saying, is that this isn't something which these men do from time to time," Will replied. "They must be getting a whole lot of money to keep this operation going, which means that we have to be extra careful. I hate to think what would happen to us if they caught us."

"Let's get a closer look," Amy suggested as she saw two men lowering a dinghy into the water. Without waiting for a response, she hurried down the hill.

By the time the children arrived at the beach, the dinghy was beached on the sand and the men had disappeared from sight.

"Where do you think they've gone?" Sarah asked.

"I don't know, but the only reason someone would land here would be to deliver information, bring something, or take something," Joe said. "And since we know paintings are being taken, it would seem most logical if they came here to take the paintings away to sell them."

From the shelter of the bushes, the children watched as two men from the trees. Judging from the clothes that they wore, they assumed they were the pilot and the co-pilot. Both of them were carrying a number of rolled-up objects.

"They must be the paintings," Will said.

Reaching the dingy, the men took the oars and rowed. When they got to the seaplane, they climbed out and disappeared inside with the objects. A few moments later, the men stepped back into the dinghy and rowed back to the shore. After pulling the dinghy up against the sand, they headed in the direction of the woods.

Will waited till he was sure that the men had disappeared into the trees before he spoke. "I just thought of something."

"What?" Sarah asked.

"One of us could hide aboard that seaplane and, when it lands, tell the police about what is happening on this island," Will said.

Joe nodded. "That could work."

"But we don't have any idea of where the machine will fly to," Amy said.

"Anywhere is better than here. We haven't seen any boats pass close by, except for that sole police boat and, with the Lazy Lucy sunk, we have to take a chance. But we have to make a decision fast." Will looked at the others. "Can anyone think of a better suggestion?"

Joe thought for a moment. "No, but who would go?"

"It should be me or you," Will replied. "And, since I thought of the plan, I'll go." He stood up and looked at Joe. "I'll need you to come with me so you can row the dinghy back."

"What can I do?" Amy asked.

"I'll need you and Sarah to head for the cabin and keep watch," Will said. "Let us know the moment you see someone coming."

CHAPTER 16

DESTINATION UNKNOWN

As the girls raced off, the boys headed for the dinghy. Climbing in, Will took the oars and rowed as hard as he could. The seaplane wasn't a great distance away, so it didn't take too long to get there.

"Good luck," Joe said as Will stepped onto the machine.

"Thanks, I'll need it," Will replied. "Oh, it might be helpful if you listen to the men from time to time. If I do get captured, the pilot is likely to contact them somehow."

Joe nodded. "Let's hope that never happens."

Will turned and disappeared inside the machine. Joe grabbed the oars and rowed back. Glancing back towards the beach, he spotted the girls racing in his direction.

As the dinghy touched the sand, Amy yelled out. "Hurry!"

Joe followed the girls towards the nearest bush and lay down just seconds before the two men emerged from the woods and walked across the sand.

As they rowed towards the seaplane, Joe looked at the girls. "That was close."

"I hope Will found a good place to hide," Sarah said.

"We'll soon find out," Amy said. "If they start the engines and fly away, we'll know they didn't see him."

The children waited anxiously as the men got ready to depart. The engines started and the propellers spun around. A moment later, the seaplane taxied across the water, gathering speed as it did so. It rose above the water, climbed for half a minute, and banked to the right.

~

Will felt a bump as the machine hit the water. It taxied for a minute or so before it stopped and the engines were switched off.

Not daring to move, Will listened carefully. With any luck, the men would leave and come back for the paintings later. That way, he could take the paintings and show them to the police. He had no idea where he was had the aircraft had been travelling for some time, but he was sure it wouldn't take too long to notify the police.

While he was thinking, the men's voices suddenly got louder. Will held his breath. He could hear them close by and he heard objects being moved. Then, he heard the footsteps move away and, a moment later, the plane tipped slightly. He assumed it was the men stepping off and, as the voices got quieter, he realised he was right.

He waited a bit longer before he peeled back the rug and stood up. He knew they would be on water, but he didn't know if it would be a lake or the sea.

The cabin windows were so dirty that he had to take the rug and wipe a spot clean before he could see through them. Once this was done, he dropped the rug and peered through.

The plane was moored against a pier by the side of a large lake. He couldn't see anyone for a moment, and he wondered where the men had disappeared to. He then heard a car as it spluttered to life. Looking around, he saw dust spiral into the air as a vehicle roared down a dirt track.

Satisfied that both men were probably in the car, he examined the machine. The paintings were missing, just as he had expected. Unfortunately, there was nothing else that the police would be interested in, so he hurried to the front of the plane.

After opening the door, he stepped onto the pier and looked around. He noticed that the woods encircled almost the entire lake. It looked like a very desolate spot.

Even though the sun was shining, a cold breeze was blowing across the lake. Rubbing his hands together in an attempt get keep warm, he walked quickly towards the woods.

Arriving at the dirt track that the vehicle had gone down, he started walking along it. After a while, he was glad to see it joined with a bigger road.

Suddenly, he heard a noise. It was a car heading towards him along the main road. The noise of the engine got louder as it approached and Will waved his arms.

The vehicle whizzed past, the driver obviously not seeing him. Will raced onto the road and waved his hands at the disappearing car. He hoped that the driver would glance in his rear-view mirror and stop, but this did not happen.

As the vehicle rounded a bend and disappeared from view, Will put his hands down. He had been just a few seconds too late.

With his hands in his pockets, he went down the

road in the direction that the car had come from. He knew it was still relatively early, but he hoped there would be more cars coming soon.

Will continued walking for ten minutes until he had reached an intersection. Except for that very first one, he hadn't even heard a vehicle, let alone seen one.

He walked up to the signpost and stared at the names of the towns in disbelief. They didn't at all look like British names! He had assumed he was in England or Scotland, but now he knew he wasn't. He suddenly saw a name that he recognised and gasped. He was in France!

He should have realised that it was the obvious place. A painting could be stolen at night in London and be sold at noon in Paris before it was even discovered to be missing.

Hearing a noise, he turned around and saw a car coming towards him. Smiling, he stepped out into the middle of the road and waved his arms to and fro.

The vehicle slowed down and Joe hurried over to the driver's side. "Do you speak English?"

"Yes, why?" the man said, speaking English with a thick French accent.

Will's face broke into a smile. "I need to go to the police station. Can you take me there?"

The man frowned. "Why do you want to go there?"

"I need tell the police about some men who are stealing paintings," Will replied.

The man looked shocked for a moment or two, but then he smiled. "Climb in the back and I'll drive you to the nearest town."

"Thanks heaps." Will opened the passenger side door and saw that there was a person sitting in the back. He stared into the man's eyes and froze. It was the pilot of the seaplane!

Startled, Will stepped backwards. Before the man could say anything, he turned and raced away. He heard a door open as the man yelled out. "Hey! Come back!"

Will looked back and saw that both men had climbed out of the vehicle and were hurrying towards him. He could see that their expressions had now changed and he regretted having told them why he wanted the police.

However, there was nothing he could do about it now. He arrived at the woods and ran past trees and bushes, his mind in a whirl. How could he have been so stupid? He should have made sure that the men weren't the crooks before he told them his tale.

Will could hear twigs snap and branches break as the two men chased him through the woods. Unfortunately, the woods weren't really thick enough to lose his pursuers. He continued on for three or so minutes, but still they chased him.

Glancing around, he saw they were gaining ground. He would have to leave the woods and try another tactic. Heading towards the road, he was soon at the edge of the trees. Pausing for a moment, he caught sight of some cows that were grazing in the field opposite.

He tore across the road to the fence. Climbing through it, he glanced back to see if the men were still following him, which they were. He ran past the cows, most of which took little notice of him, but then he caught sight of a bull that was looking at him.

Slowing down, he looked away and tried to hide behind the various cows that he passed. But when there were no more cows, he saw that the bull was still there. And it was closer.

Seeing that the fence was just up ahead, he knew

what he had to do. Pausing for a moment to get his breath back, he saw that the men were closing in.

They started shouting, and Will realised they hadn't even noticed the bull. As the animal looked towards the men, he knew this was his one and only chance.

He ran towards the fence just as the bull trotted towards the men. Will didn't look back as he ran, but when he heard a number of shouts, he knew that they had seen the bull.

However, he didn't stop running. He knew that as soon as the bull wanted to, the animal could charge after him, so he ran like the wind. Not until he climbed through the fence did he pause and look across the field.

As he did so, a shot was heard and the bull, which was quite close to one of the men, turned around and bolted. Will assumed that the other man, who had reached the fence, had fired a gun into the air to scare the animal away.

As the second man limped towards his friend, Will knew that he would never have a better chance to escape. With a newfound respect for bulls, he gazed around at the surrounding area and saw that there was a field of corn growing quite close by, just across a small stream.

There was a road on the other side of the field and, even better, what looked like a vehicle was parked on the edge of it.

Hoping that help was not far away, Will walked to the stream, jumped over it, and hurried through the corn field. He glanced back from time to time, but couldn't hear or see anyone. Maybe, just maybe, the chase was over.

As Will walked between the plants which were just below his height, he was tempted to pick some corn as he was hungry, but he resisted the temptation and continued on.

Will hadn't glimpsed his pursuers since the incident with the bull so, as he reached the other end of the field and walked towards the vehicle beside the road, he relaxed.

He caught sight of an old man and his dog sitting in the car and was just about to wave at them when a noise startled him. Looking left, he saw dust swirl around as a car roared down the road.

Will paused for just a moment as the car stopped and out climbed his pursuers. They saw him at once and gave chase.

Will turned and raced back into the corn field. He knew that the men would soon overtake him, so he would have to try something else. He quickly dropped to the ground and began crawling. It was hard on his hands and knees but, if he could confuse the men, he might get lucky and escape.

Moving as silently as he could, he heard the men stop. A moment later, he heard two sets of noises in different directions and realised they had separated.

Knowing that he could never outrun someone on his knees, Will paused and stayed as silent as he could. As long as the man didn't crawl about like he was doing, the chance of him finding him was small. Will waited until the sound was far away before he continued crawling.

Suddenly, there was a rustling noise and the corn stalks in front of him parted, revealing the face of the pilot.

Will leapt to his feet, but before he could run, the second man appeared from the other side and he knew that he was trapped. Seeing that there was a pistol tucked into the man's trousers, he raised his hands in surrender.

"Thought you could escape, hey?" the pilot said, grinning as he led the way out of the corn field. "I thought I'd try something smart and stay where I was for a minute or two, and it paid off."

"You got lucky," Will said.

"Not at all. If we hadn't caught you here we would have caught you somewhere else." The pilot laughed as he dragged Will towards the car.

CHAPTER 17

NOW OR NEVER

The girls and Joe were talking amongst themselves by the tent when Joe paused and frowned as he heard a sound rising and falling on the wind. He took the binoculars and peered through them.

Nothing could be seen at first, but then he saw a speck in the sky. "The seaplane is returning."

Amy stood up as the machine approached. "Are you sure it's the same one that landed here?"

Joe nodded. "It looks to be the same." He fell silent as the plane turned towards the inlet. "Let's go and see what happens."

They hurried towards the place where the seaplane had taken off from only a few hours ago.

As they arrived and hid behind the bushes, they saw the two pilots rowing the dinghy towards the shore. In between them was Will.

"So they caught him." Joe punched his fist against the palm of his other hand angrily. "That's not good."

"I wonder how," Sarah piped up.

"Let's go to the cabin and see if we can find out," Joe suggested.

They waited for the men to land and head towards the woods before they followed them. They didn't want to go too close in case they were spotted, so they were just nearing the cabin when they saw the men leave.

Joe and the girls knelt down to avoid being seen. Once they were out of hearing, Amy spoke. "I wonder where they're going."

"Back to the plane by the looks of it," Joe said.

"Are they going to take off?" Sarah asked.

"Let's go and see." Joe followed the path that the men had taken and paused at the edge of the woods. He was just in time to see the men rowing to the plane.

Within a matter of minutes, the machine had roared to life and was taxiing across the water. Once it had enough speed, it lifted off and banked to the left.

"I wonder if they're going back to where they came from," Joe said.

"Probably," Amy replied.

"I don't think so," Joe said. "They were headed in the direction of the mainland when they flew off just then, but when the plane flew in, it appeared to come from across the water. Anyway, it doesn't really matter where they've gone, we should be seeing what the men are doing to Will."

"You're right." Amy followed Joe and Sarah back into the woods.

They couldn't hear anything, but as Kenneth left the cabin, they followed him. He hurried along the beach. The children tried to keep up with him without being seen, but when they rounded a bend, he was nowhere to be seen.

"I wonder where he went," Amy said.

"Well, if we stay here, he might return." Joe left the beach and found someplace near the bushes where they could see the entire inlet. He sat and waited.

Less than ten minutes had passed before Sarah saw

the man in a rowboat. "He must have gone to get that."

"Yes, it must have been hidden in one of the caves." Joe watched as Kenneth beached the craft on the sand and disappeared into the woods. He turned to the girls. "If one of us hid in that rowboat, they could find the police when it lands and get them to come here. It could be our last chance to get help."

"Would that rowboat be big enough to hide someone in it?" Amy said, sceptical.

"Maybe not me or you, but I think Sarah would fit." Joe looked at Sarah. "I know it's risky, but it's a risk that needs to be taken."

"I could go," Amy volunteered. "I know I'm a bit taller but—"

"I'll be fine," Sarah interrupted. "After all, I did climb up the side of that boat the other week, and that was much harder than hiding in a rowboat."

"Hiding in the rowboat is only the beginning," Joe said. "You'll have to get to the nearest police station. And that will be especially hard since we don't where the man will row to. Hopefully, it won't be too far from a village, but you never know."

"Shall I tell the first person I see?" Sarah asked.

"Yes, but count to two hundred before you climb out of the rowboat," Joe said. "You can't wait too long in case the man comes back, but if you climb out too soon he might see you."

"So now we just wait," Amy said.

Joe nodded. "Yes. It shouldn't be too long, though."

Shortly, Kenneth emerged from the woods. Joe's heart beat fast as he waited for the man to approach. As soon as it was certain that he was going to the rowboat, he stood up and brushed past the bushes until he was standing on the sand.

He gazed down, all the while keeping one eye turned

towards the man. He wanted to give the impression that he hadn't seen him. Hearing a yell, he looked up.

Kenneth was hurrying towards him. "Hey! I want to have a talk with you."

Even though the man was smiling, Joe knew that he was trying to trick him. But, since it was he who was trying to trick the man, it would work in his favour to make the man believe that he wasn't going to run away. So he stayed still, waiting until the last possible moment.

Just as Kenneth slowed down, Joe took off running. With a yell, the man raced after him. Joe ran along the sand, through the bushes, and onto the grass. While Kenneth was still making his way through the undergrowth, Joe hurried into the woods.

Joe heard the man yell out once more as he ran past the trees and hoped that he would be able to lose him in the thick woods. He didn't want to keep on running forever and so, once he thought that he had a good lead, he paused behind a large pine tree and waited. He crouched down and listened for any sound that would indicate that the man was close.

But he didn't hear anything. Joe's heart beat fast. He didn't know if this meant that the man had given up or if he was doing what he was doing. Joe sat still and listened.

A number of minutes passed and he relaxed. It looked as though the man had given up. But, just as he rose to his feet, the sound of a twig being stepped on could be heard. He froze.

~

As the beady-eyed man followed Joe into the woods, Sarah and Amy emerged from the bushes and hurried towards the rowboat.

"Hurry up!" Amy whispered to Sarah as she raced along. She had no idea how much time they would have and, if they didn't succeed this time, there was no way that they could try a second time using the rowboat. It was now or never.

Reaching the craft, Amy turned towards the bushes. No one could be seen. Turning back, she noticed that the rowboat was pretty big, one of the largest that she had seen. A tarpaulin covered the rear half of it.

After stepping into it, she and Sarah pulled away the tarpaulin. Underneath were a number of boxes.

"I wonder what's in them," Sarah said.

"I don't know, but it doesn't matter. Let's take out enough so that you can hide." Amy grabbed a box and carried it to the bushes.

Sarah did the same and soon all that remained was one box. "We'll need to leave this one else the man will know something is wrong."

Amy nodded. "Let's hope there's enough room. Climb in and see."

Sarah stepped in and sat down at the rear of the rowboat. She put her legs as close together as possible. "I can't get any tighter."

Amy frowned. "It will have to do. It should be fine." She moved the sole box as close to Sarah's feet as possible and started to put the tarpaulin over it and her sister. "Take care and good luck."

"Thanks." Sarah's voice was muffled as Amy covered her face with the tarpaulin.

Once Amy had finished, she glanced back towards the beach. No one was about. She quickly ran towards the bushes. After reaching them, she sat down and waited.

CHAPTER 18

BICYCLE MADNESS

Joe grabbed a stick and prepared to trip the man up as he walked past. He waited and waited, but nothing happened. He couldn't stand the suspense, so he peered around. He dropped the stick and smiled with relief.

It was a rabbit. The animal raced off into the bushes. Joe sighed and hurried towards the beach. He thought he had given the girls enough time, but he would soon see if he was right.

~

Amy watched with bated breath as Kenneth climbed into the rowboat, grabbed the oars, and started rowing. There was nothing to indicate that he knew what was hidden underneath the tarpaulin at the rear of the boar, and she hoped that it would stay like that for the whole journey. Hearing a rustling noise behind her, she spotted Joe emerging from the bushes.

"Did she get in okay?" Joe asked. Amy nodded and handed him the binoculars so that he could see for himself. He saw that the craft was steadily getting further and further away from the island. "Let's hope the man doesn't need to pull away that tarpaulin."

"Well, if we see the rowboat coming back soon, it'll probably mean that Sarah's been discovered," Amy said.

The two children stood side by side as they watched the craft get further and further away. Soon, all that could be seen was a tiny speck. Then, even that was gone.

Amy turned to Joe. "So, what do we do now?"

~

Sarah stayed as silent as a mouse as the man rowed. She had no way of knowing which way they were going, but since Kenneth hadn't discovered her, she assumed he was heading for the mainland.

Time seemed to stand still as she listened to the waves lapping against the side of the boat. She could hear her heart beating fast, and wondered if the man would hear it. She resisted the urge to cough and, as the rowboat came to stop, she wondered if they had arrived.

A moment later, she got her answer. The boat creaked as Kenneth stood up and climbed out. As least, she assumed he did, but she couldn't be certain. She listened as hard as she could, but all she could hear was the calling of seabirds. She then heard the sound of a car engine.

Lying still, she quietly counted to two hundred. It seemed a long time, and she was tempted to move sooner, but she wanted to follow Joe's orders, so she stayed there until she had finished counting.

She then pulled back the tarpaulin and stood up. Glancing around, she saw the rowboat was moored next to some rocks in a small inlet that was bordered by a cliff. It was from these cliffs that seagulls soared in the sky above.

She looked towards the land and realised she would have to climb over a number of rocks to get to the sand. From there, a narrow path led up the cliff face. She paused for a moment or two so she could make certain she couldn't hear the man.

She couldn't, so she hurried towards the rocks. Her legs were a bit stiff after being cooped up in such a tight space, but she was able to cross the rocks without slipping.

After reaching the sand, she hurried up the path. As she neared the top, she slowed down. She had no idea what lay at the top of the cliff and she didn't want to be caught by surprise.

The path came out next to a deserted dirt road. Sarah had no idea which way the nearest town was, but looking to the right, she caught sight of a house half hidden by trees.

She crossed the road and walked towards it. Not knowing how far the nearest police station would be, she had to find someone who would help her. Though there didn't appear to be a single soul around, there was a chance there would be someone in the house who could help her.

Sarah was almost at the front door when it suddenly swung open. Her heart caught in her throat. It was Kenneth!

She turned and raced away as fast as she could. She didn't glance back, but she could tell by the footsteps that, after a moment's hesitation, the man had started chasing her.

She was so angry with herself. She had assumed he would have a car waiting on the mainland and would drive away in it as soon as he had left the boat.

But this obviously had not happened. Glancing

back, she could see that he was gaining. In another fifteen seconds or so, he would be able to reach out and grab her.

As she reached the road, she changed direction and rushed into the woods. She twisted and turned as she pushed past bushes, not taking notice of the scratches that she was getting.

She looked back and saw that the plump man was having more difficulty getting through the bushes than she was. She was quite confident of evading capture, but then the woods started to thin out and, before she knew it, she was on the other side. Pausing for a moment, she saw there was a small village nestled next to the coast in the valley below.

Sarah knew that she would have to find some transport if she was to reach the police station before the man caught her, so she scanned the fields below as she ran down the hill.

~

Amy and Joe gazed through the bushes. In front of them was the cabin. The only window was on the same side as them, so they could look through it and see Will, who was sitting on a chair.

Joe watched as the boss paced back and forth while the man with the ponytail stood in front of Will. "We'll need to cause a distraction if we're to get him out of there."

"Like what?" Amy said.

"I don't know," Joe admitted. "But I can't think of any other way that would get Will released."

Amy suddenly grinned. "Hey, I just thought of something."

"What?" Joe asked.

"We could do a swap," Amy suggested.

"But we don't have anything that the men want," Joe complained.

"Not yet," Amy said.

Joe frowned as he looked at his younger sister. "What are you thinking of?"

~

As Sarah ran down the hill, she caught sight of a family lying in the shade of a big oak tree. As luck would have it, several bicycles lay on the ground near them.

Glancing back, she saw that the lead that she had managed to get while she was in the woods was rapidly decreasing. She had to get to a bicycle quickly. Her legs were burning with fatigue and she was breathing heavily, but she couldn't give up now. The others were depending on her to get to the police and she didn't want to let them down.

She finally reached the bicycles. After grabbing the smallest one, she climbed on the machine and hurriedly pedalled away. Seeing a narrow path that ran along the side of a field before going down a small hill and into the village, she took it.

She glanced back and saw that Kenneth had also grabbed one of the bicycles and was riding after her. She turned back and whipped the wheel to the right to avoid a pot hole. The gradual downward slope increased the bicycle's speed and soon it seemed as though she was flying along.

The shops came into view as she neared the hill and she realised the village was roughly the same size as Smugglers Cove.

Hearing a noise, she looked back and saw that the man was right on her tail. She hadn't really expected him to give up, but obviously he had recognised her from the island and realised what she was trying to do.

It would be so annoying to fail so close to her objective, so she took a deep breath and pedalled furiously. The bicycle sped down the hill, going faster than she had ever gone before.

She didn't glance back to see what the man was doing but assumed he had also realised how close to the village they were and had also increased his speed.

The path took a sharp right hand turn at the bottom of the hill and though Sarah slowed down, she didn't slow down as much as she normally would.

The tires on the bicycle screeched over the stones as she came to the road and she grabbed on the brakes. The bicycle flew around the corner too fast, and she was lucky to make the corner as she swept into the main street and headed towards the harbour.

The bicycle slowly increased speed and Sarah realised that the brakes weren't working. "Oh no!" She flew down the street, getting faster and faster.

CHAPTER 19

IN PLAIN SIGHT

Joe stood on the beach beside the two caves. "I don't understand. We've searched both of these and there's nothing in them."

"There must be," Amy stated. "Where else would they be storing the paintings? Remember, the first time we saw one of the men he was around here, and he disappeared. He's not likely to go into an empty cave for nothing."

She entered the first cave and, using her torch, led the way around. She made sure to inspect every hidey hole. The two of them left the first cave after five minutes and entered the second one. This one was smaller than the first and it took even less time to search.

As Amy left the cave and stood on the beach, she switched off the torch, disappointed. "I thought they would be in there."

"I'm sure there's another way to distract the men," Joe said.

Amy shook her head. "No. This isn't just about rescuing Will."

"No?" Joe repeated.

Amy sat down on the sand. "If that man comes back

from the mainland and tells the others about Sarah, what do you think will happen?"

"They'll leave on the seaplane as soon as they can and take the paintings with them," Joe said.

Amy nodded. "Yes. Which means if we find the paintings, we can delay them. I just wish there was some way of knowing where that man went."

Joe suddenly grinned. "I've got it! Pretend to be the man."

"What?" Amy said, confused.

"I'll go to the bushes where we were the other day, and you can walk along the beach," Joe replied. "If I wave left, you go left. If I wave right, you go right, okay?"

"What will this prove?" Amy asked.

"I want to know the exact location of the man before he disappeared," Joe said. "So get into position." He turned and raced towards the bushes.

Before long, he was in position. Waving for Amy to start walking, he waited. As she got closer to him, he waved her right, and then left.

After five minutes of stepping this way and that, Joe joined his sister on the beach. Standing where she was, he gazed around. He was close to the caves but, surprisingly, neither of the two were opposite him. He frowned.

Amy turned to him. "So what did this prove? We know the man went into one of the two caves, so—"

"Or so we thought," Joe interrupted.

"What do you mean?" Amy asked.

Joe waved his hands in front of him. "Where are we standing?"

Amy frowned. "In front of the two caves."

Joe smiled. "Be more specific."

Amy looked again and suddenly realised that while

she was standing in front of the two caves, she was actually standing between the two caves. "Are you thinking what I'm thinking?"

Joe nodded. "We searched the caves, but we didn't search the bushes between the caves." He hurried forward and the two of them were soon at the bushes. It didn't take long before he let out a yell. He flung aside a pile of brush to reveal a tunnel.

"Golly!" Amy looked at Joe. "You were right."

"Let's see what's in here." Switching the torch on, Joe entered the tunnel. Amy was right behind him and, after she replaced the brush in its correct place, followed Joe.

~

As Sarah whipped down the street on the runaway bicycle, Kenneth shot past on his machine. Startled, she grimly smiled. Obviously, his brakes weren't working either. And, since he had been going faster down the hill, the extra weight made him whip past her. She only caught a glimpse of the man's face, but she could see he looked scared.

The two bicycles sped down the road. Luckily, there were not many people walking along the street, and those who were, quickly leapt out of the way when they saw the bicycles approach.

Sarah was trying her hardest to spot a police officer, but she couldn't see one. She knew there would be a police station, she would just have to find it before she got caught.

She thought about crashing the bicycle deliberately, but didn't want to risk hurting herself, so she just followed the man down the road.

Just up ahead lay the harbour. It was a sharp turn

and she didn't know whether or not the man, at the speed he was going, would make it. He didn't. She watched as the front tire of his bicycle hit the concrete and he catapulted into the air.

"Yes!" Sarah couldn't help but utter a shout of joy as she saw the man hit the water and disappear from view.

The smile disappeared from her face as she approached the corner. Grabbing the handlebars as hard as she could, she waited until the right moment before she whipped them to the left.

The tires screeched on the gravel as the machine neared the water. She thought she had just enough room and then she realised she was going to suffer the same fate as the man. The bicycle hit the concrete and she flew up into the air. She hit the water and sank beneath the waves.

Sarah swam upwards and, a few moments later, broke through the surface. Glancing around, she spotted the man swimming powerfully towards the pier. Her only hope would be to reach it before him.

She was closer to it than he was and she swam as fast as she could. Fortunately, there was a teenage boy walking down the pier who reached out his hand and helped her up. "Where's the police station?"

The boy pointed. "It's halfway up that street. Why, is something wrong?"

Sarah glanced behind her and spotted her pursuer pulling himself up onto the pier. "I need to get there before he does."

The boy smiled. "Leave it to me."

Sarah left the boy and ran off in the direction of the police station. She didn't know what the boy had meant when he had said that he would help, but as she raced down the street, she heard a yell.

She looked behind her and saw Kenneth lying facedown on the pier. The boy smiled and hurried off. She didn't know what had happened. Maybe the boy had tripped him, but it didn't matter. The man stumbled to his feet and hurried after her, limping.

Sarah was used to running around, but it was clear that the man wasn't, and the chase was taking its toll on him. But she didn't feel sorry for him. He was a crook and he deserved what he got.

Sarah raced down the street. Reaching the halfway point, she saw the police station. "Yes!" With a smile, she walked up the steps and went inside.

~

With Joe leading the way, Amy followed him down the tunnel, which widened into a cave. As Joe shone the torch around the space, he could see why the man had come in here.

There were boxes stacked by the walls and a table and chairs in the middle. On the table was a lamp and a number of papers.

Upon examination they saw that it was a pile of maps. Spreading one out, Joe saw that it was a map of England. "I wonder what these circles mean."

"Maybe they are towns that the men have robbed from," Amy suggested as she left Joe and walked over to the boxes.

"If so, these men have been busy. Really busy." After folding the map up and leaving it in the same condition in which he had found it, Joe joined Amy as she pulled out a tin.

"Hey, it's baked beans," Amy said, surprised.

Joe reached into the box and pulled out another tin of food. "This one is peaches." He shone his torch at the box and they were amazed at how many tins were there. "Phew. That's a lot of food."

Amy glanced towards the other boxes. "Especially if those contain food as well."

"They must be planning to be here for a long time." Amy looked around the cave. "Do you see paintings or anything that might be stolen?"

Joe shook his head. "The paintings would probably get damp in here, so they would have to be somewhere dry."

"But they're not in the cabin or the church, and they are the only buildings except for the ruined ones—" Amy said.

"They have to be in the lighthouse," Joe interrupted. "It's the only answer. It's dry inside."

"But how do we get in?" Amy asked.

"Let's wait and see if one of the men goes there," Joe suggested. "It should be low tide soon, so if we hurry to the woods, we might catch sight of someone heading to the lighthouse."

Joe and Amy had been sitting by the woods for roughly half an hour when the man with the ponytail and glasses appeared. The children ducked down as Luke walked past them and headed towards the lighthouse.

"Looks like I was right," Joe said.

But what do we do now?" Amy asked.

Joe waited as Luke walked across the rocks. Once the man had reached the building, he took a key from his pocket and unlocked the door.

"Now's our chance," Joe said.

"But how do we get in without him seeing us?" Amy asked.

Joe hurried towards the rocks. "We have to hope he has gone up the stairs for some reason."

The two of them climbed over the rocks as fast as they could. While low tide had passed, the water hadn't yet started to rise, so they were able to cross to the lighthouse without getting wet.

Joe slowed down as they reached the building. He put his ear as close to the door as possible and listened. No sound could be heard. He looked at Amy. "Get ready to run in case he's still down below."

As Amy nodded, Joe grabbed the door handle. He hoped it would be unlocked, but if the man had locked it again, they would be unable to get in.

CHAPTER 20

INSIDE THE LIGHTHOUSE

The door opened without any trouble. Stepping inside, Joe saw that the place was quite old. Also, the spiral stairway was bigger than he thought it would be.

Amy looked around. "No sign of the man."

Joe shook his head. "No. Let's go upstairs and see if there's somewhere to hide."

They went up the stairs. They had yet to reach a room when they heard footsteps. The man was coming down the stairs!

Joe hurriedly glanced around. "Shall we go up or down?"

"Up," Amy replied. "We should be close to one of the rooms."

The two of them hurried up the stairs as fast as they could, hoping the sounds of their footsteps would blend in with the man's.

Joe looked up and caught sight of Luke above him and realised they were not going to make it in time. "Blow!" They raced back down the steps until they came to the door. Joe opened it, but paused.

"What's wrong?" Amy whispered.

"I just thought of something." After closing the door, Joe hurried to the back of the steps and crouched down. He motioned for Amy to do the same, and they sat in silence as Luke came into view ten seconds later.

Without looking behind him, the man opened the door, closed it, and locked it. Joe couldn't actually see him lock it, but as he heard the key turn, he knew what had happened. Listening, he heard the footsteps of the man fade away. "Let's hope we haven't got locked in here for nothing."

"I'm sure the paintings are here somewhere," Amy said. "Where else could they be?"

Joe glanced around. "Well, they're not down here. Let's head up."

This time, the two of them walked instead of running. They were soon at a door. Finding it unlocked, Joe opened it. He smiled. In front of him were a number of packages that were tubular in shape. "Those look like the packages that the pilots took this morning."

Amy frowned. "But if these are the paintings, why wouldn't they have taken all of them?"

"Well, maybe they only deliver the ones that people have paid for." Joe picked one up and saw that it had a name tag on it. It read: The Blue Lotus.

"Is that the name of a painting?" Amy questioned.

"I don't know. Let's open it and see." Joe undid the string and, with Amy's help, unravelled what had been packed inside the paper.

"Yes!" Amy exclaimed in jubilation as she saw a beautiful painting of a lotus flower. "I wonder how much it's worth."

Joe spotted a name on the corner of the painting. Bending down, he read what it said. "Vincent van Gough. Hey, I think I've heard of him."

Amy nodded. "Yes, so have I. My teacher was talking about him. If what she said was true, his paintings are worth a fortune."

"We should try to take all the ones that say Vincent van Gough then," Joe said. "We can manage two each, so that will be four."

Amy put the painting back in its protective packaging. "But how are we going to get out? Just stroll out the front door?"

"Of course, we…" Joe paused as he realised that the man had locked the door, trapping them inside. "I guess I didn't think the plan through. But at least we have the paintings."

"But what are we going to do with them?" Amy questioned.

"Well, one of the men should come back eventually, so we'll tell him about the swap then," Joe said.

"So we just wait here until that happens?" Amy asked.

Joe nodded. "Hopefully, Sarah will be back with the police before anything happens but, if not, we'll do a deal with those men."

"What if they don't agree to that deal?" Amy asked.

"Then they don't get the paintings," Joe said. "Either way, I can't see anything happening for a while, so let's explore the rest of the lighthouse."

Leaving the room, they climbed up the rest of the steps. Halfway up they came to a door. Opening it, they saw that it was a very small room with no windows and a low ceiling.

"Why does it smell weird?" Amy asked.

Joe picked up one of the many cans that were on a shelf. "It's oil." Looking around, he realised that they were all the same. "This room is packed full of cans of oil. That's why it smells."

"Why would someone need this much oil?" Amy wondered.

"To light the lamp," Joe replied. "I read somewhere

that lamps in lighthouses had to burn oil to keep alight."

"Would it be any use now?" Amy asked.

"No, I don't think so," Joe replied. "It must have been here for years and years. Goodness knows how long."

Leaving the smelly room, they kept on climbing up the stairs. There was one final room before the top, and inside that room was a mattress that had clearly seen better days, some matches, and a lamp.

They climbed up the final few steps until they reached the very top of the building, which was the lamp room. It had big windows all around. The view was magnificent. A massive lamp stood in the middle of the room. Broken glass lay on the floor, so they had to be careful where they walked.

Joe examined the lamp. "This probably hasn't worked in years and years."

Amy opened the door and stepped out onto the gallery. She clutched onto the railing and looked down. It was a long way. She felt dizzy even just looking at the ground.

Whipping her head away, she followed Joe as they walked in a circle around the structure. Since they were so high, they could see for miles and miles.

Finishing up where they started a few moments later, Amy glanced towards the beach. "Can you see the cabin? I can't."

"No, I can't see it either. It's in a pretty good hiding place. I doubt you could see it from an aeroplane either." Joe suddenly clutched his sister's arm. "Look!"

As Amy saw one of the men appear near the woods, she frowned. "I wonder where he's going."

Both of them soon discovered the answer as the man left the grass and walked onto the rocks.

"Oh no, why is he coming back so soon?" Amy

asked.

"I don't know, but why does he have a rucksack on his back? Unless…" Joe looked over at his sister. "He's come to take the paintings away."

"So, we're finished," Amy muttered.

"Not yet. Follow me." Joe hurried into the lamp room and raced down the steps. Puffing, he arrived on the ground floor half a minute later. He hurried over to some wooden boxes that were lined up against the walls. Trying to lift one, he realised it was too heavy. "Help me lift this."

"But—" Amy said.

"Just help me!" Joe interrupted.

Amy helped him as they moved the box to the door and placed it down in front of it. Joe ran to get another box as footsteps were heard outside.

"Hurry! One more." Joe hurried over to the next box and they dragged it across the floor. Just as he heard the sound of the key sliding into the lock, the box slid next to the other one.

"Lean against the door," Joe instructed. "We can't let the man open it."

The two of them leaned against the door just as the key turned and the door was pushed open. It moved a small bit, but then stopped.

A moment later, the man yelled out. "Hey! What's going on?"

CHAPTER 21

KABOOM!

Joe motioned for Amy to be quiet as they stood there, not daring to move. Joe didn't want to give any indication that it was just two children that were stopping the man. He smiled as he thought of an idea. In his best grownup voice, he started speaking. "How long until the four police boats arrive?"

Amy grinned. Hoping that the man would believe them, she copied Joe and began speaking in an adult voice. "It shouldn't be too long. Though the army will probably arrive first."

"You're right," Joe said. "The fifty paratroopers should be circling the island now."

"Let's not forget about the two destroyers," Amy said.

"Ah, yes. I just received word they're on schedule. Should be here in thirty minutes. If only those men knew what was about to happen. They'll have no chance to escape." Joe stopped speaking and put a finger to his lips, motioning Amy to be quiet.

They heard hurried footsteps and then silence. After waiting for a minute, they moved a box away and tried to open the door. But they couldn't. The man had locked it again.

"Well, at least he didn't get in," Joe said.

"But we didn't get out either." Amy giggled. "I could hardly keep a straight face, especially when you talked about the paratroopers."

Joe laughed as he thought about the conversation that they had just had. "Me too. Though, I think you went a bit far with the two destroyers."

"I just said whatever came into my head," Amy said. "Hey, hadn't we better see if the man is heading to the cabin?"

"Yes, though we can't leave this unguarded," Joe said. "We'll have to split up. I'll stay here while you see."

Amy hurried up the steps. Joe went over to the sealed wooden boxes and felt around for the lightest one. He slowly dragged it across the floor until it was firmly up against the others. He was resting on it when Amy appeared.

After sitting down next to him, she explained what she had seen. "I was just in time to see the man disappear into the woods. I waited for a minute or so, but he didn't come into view, so I expect he's now telling the others about the destroyers, police boats—"

"And the paratroopers," Joe interrupted. "Good work. I managed to move one box, but we'll need to move more if we're to stop those men."

~

As Will sat on the chair with his hands behind his back, he wondered what the others were up to. He hadn't let the men know anything about what he or the others knew or suspected, but he realised that sooner or later the men would find out the truth.

Marvin was pacing back and forth when Luke threw open the door and rushed in. He had a wild look on his face as he rushed towards him. "We need to scramble. The destroyers will be here in thirty minutes."

Marvin stared at him. "What are you talking about?"

Luke quickly explained, his words rushing out all at once. "I went to the lighthouse to have a look at the paintings just like you told me to do, but I couldn't open the door."

Marvin frowned. "What do you mean, you couldn't open it?"

"There was too much weight on the other side of the door," Luke replied. "Anyway, I then I heard voices. They said that four patrol boats were coming, fifty paratroopers, and two destroyers. We need to split, boss. Whatever happens, I can't go to jail again."

"Destroyers? Paratroopers?" Marvin laughed. "I don't know who said that, but they fooled you. There's no way they would be interested in us. But there's one thing I would like to know – did the voices sound like children?"

Luke thought. "Well, they did sound a bit weird."

"Just like I thought." The boss walked over to Will. "It seems we've found your friends."

"I don't know what you're talking about," Will said. "There's no one else on the island. We all went on the seaplane together. I expect they're sitting inside a French police station right at this moment. If I were you—"

"You're not, so shut up!" Marvin turned to Luke. "Let's go and see if you're telling the truth."

"But what about the destroyers and—" Luke argued.

"Shut up!" Marvin turned to the boy and examined the ropes that were around his wrists. "You'll soon talk when we get back with the others."

"You can't keep me locked up forever," Will stated.

"No, but once we've finished here we'll be moving

somewhere else, somewhere far, far away." Marvin laughed and grinned at Will before slamming the door shut.

Will waited for a minute. Satisfied that the men had truly gone, he attempted to undo the ropes around his wrists. But he couldn't loosen them. It was evident that the ropes had been properly tied by someone who knew a thing or two about such things.

Despite the situation, Will chuckled grimly as he thought about the destroyers and paratroopers mentioned by Luke. There was no way that help like that was coming, so it must have been a trick played by the others. But why?

~

Joe looked over at the pile of boxes that he and Amy had placed against the door. "Do you think that will be enough?"

Amy nodded. "My arms are too tired to move more boxes, so it had better be. Why don't we lie down on that mattress we saw in the other room? It will be softer than lying here."

"Okay. It will give us time to think of what we're going to do next." Joe followed his sister up the stairs until they came to the room with the mattress.

Peering out of the sole window, Joe saw the sea. He smiled. They would be able to see if a boat passed nearby and it also provided light, so they could see without having to turn on the torch all the time.

They had been relaxing for a short time when Joe suddenly heard a noise. He sat up. "Do you hear that?"

Amy also sat up. "It must be the men."

"There's only one way to find out." Joe hurried out of the room and climbed up the steps to the lamp room.

Walking out onto the gallery, Joe and Amy looked down. They saw Marvin and Luke trying their hardest to open the door.

Luke suddenly looked up and snarled. "Hey! It's just kids."

Marvin shook his fist in anger. "Open up!"

The children didn't say anything, which seemed to make the men angrier. As they watched, they had a quick conversation. Afterwards, Marvin left while Luke stayed behind and sat down.

As Joe walked into the lamp room and down the steps, he frowned. "I wonder what they intend to do."

"Maybe to keep us locked in here until we give in," Amy said.

"Which will never happen," Joe said.

"But they don't know that," Amy replied. "Besides, what else could they do?"

Joe frowned. "We should have a look at the paintings and see if there's a bag or something that we can put some in for when we leave."

Joe searched, but couldn't find anything. Going down the stairs, he heard the men come back. With his face pressed up against the door, he was able to hear what they were saying.

"We don't want to blow the entire building up, only the door," Luke said.

"Relax, I've used this stuff hundreds of times," Marvin replied. "But, just in case, we had better stand back."

Joe heard footsteps as the men retreated and he realised what was about to happen. Rushing up the stairs, he paused to grab two paintings.

Leaving the room, he bumped into Amy who was carrying some rope. "I found this in the other room. I thought we could use it to tie the paintings together, but—"

"The men are going to blast the door open!" Joe interrupted. "We have to get out of here."

As Joe rushed up the stairs, Amy followed him. "What shall we do?"

Reaching the lamp room, they dropped the paintings and rope on the floor as they opened the door and headed out onto the gallery. Looking down, they saw that the two men were now huddled behind the rocks.

Suddenly, a loud explosion tore through the silence. The building rocked from side to side. Once the rocking had stopped, Joe sighed. "Phew! For a moment I thought we were going to tip into the sea."

"Me too. They must have used more explosives than they needed." Peering down, Amy saw that there was a massive hole where the door had been just a few moments ago. As she watched, the men started walking towards the lighthouse. Amy turned to Joe, her face one of despair. "We're trapped."

Joe shook his head. "I've got a plan." After running into the lamp room, he grabbed the rope and came back. He tied one end to the railing, made sure that it was tight, then threw the rest over the edge.

Glancing down, he saw with relief that there was just enough to reach the bottom. "I know this is risky, but it's the only thing I can think of," Joe admitted. "You go first while I delay the men."

"What about the paintings?" Amy asked.

"I'll drop them down to you before I climb down." Leaving Amy, Joe hurried down the stairs as fast as he could. He could hear the men's footsteps as they walked up and knew it would be a gamble on who would reach the oil room first.

Luckily, the men were only walking and not running,

so Joe managed to reach the room first. Throwing it open, he reached for the cans. He grabbed a can and tossed it down the stairs. He repeated this process several times. As he did so, he could hear yells from the men as they made contact with the cans.

Looking over the edge of the staircase, he saw that the men were waiting until the cans had passed them. Hoping this would give him enough time to escape, Joe rushed up the steps and into the lamp room.

Taking hold of the two paintings, he walked out onto the gallery and peered down. Seeing Amy down below, he dropped a painting over the side. He wasn't sure if the wind would blow it away, but luckily it didn't.

Amy caught it firmly in her grasp. After placing it on the ground, she held out her hands for the next one. Just like the first one, she caught this one without any problem.

Joe climbed over the railing and prepared to climb down. Hearing a noise, he realised that the men were probably at the room with the mattress.

Clutching the rope, he pushed away from the building and half climbed and half slid towards the ground. He went as fast as he could, but as Amy yelled out, he looked up to see that the men were at the railing.

"Stop or else we'll cut the rope!" Marvin yelled.

Amy looked on as Joe went faster. As he did so, Marvin grabbed the rope and, using a penknife, tried to cut the rope in half.

"Hurry!" Amy shouted.

Joe hurried, but before he could reach the bottom, the rope split in half, sending him hurtling down!

CHAPTER 22

SWISS FAMILY ROBINSON STYLE

Luckily, Joe was only a few feet from the bottom and he wasn't injured.

"Just you wait!" Marvin yelled. He waved his fist before he and Luke disappeared from view.

Joe turned to Amy and reached for one of the paintings. "We'll have to run like we've never run before. If it looks like one of us will be caught, the other has to take the paintings and escape."

Joe hurried towards the rocks. Leaping over them, he had to take care since the water was slowly rising.

Suddenly, a big wave appeared and crashed against the rocks in front of them. Joe skidded to a stop as the water rushed over the rocks. "Careful, they'll be slippery now." Going slowly, he made his way over the rocks and onto dry land.

Looking back to see if Amy was safe, he caught sight of the men as they emerged from the lighthouse. Confident that the men would have to slow down just like they had, he turned and hurried into the woods with Amy close behind.

~

It had taken a while, but as Amy and Joe rested on top

of the hill, they were confident that they had lost the men.

"So, what do we do now?" Amy asked.

"We need to hide someplace where we can be safe from the men, but still know what's going on," Joe said.

"Hey, I just thought of something," Amy exclaimed. "If all the men are out searching, they might leave Will unguarded. If so, it would be the perfect time to help him escape."

Joe nodded. "If we can evade the men getting there, it might work." He looked towards the inlet. "Once that seaplane comes back, there will be two more men that we will have to deal with. So now would be the best time."

"If not, we can still try to do a swap," Amy suggested.

"Yes, we could, but I don't really want to give the paintings up that easily. If we were to get Will, we would have him and the paintings." Joe stood up. "Let's get going." He frowned as he saw something in the water. As it came closer he realised what it was. "It's the rowboat."

"Where?" Amy asked.

Joe pointed towards the inlet and Amy saw that he was right. They watched as the rowboat pulled up against the beach. Jumping out, Kenneth hurried up the sand.

Joe smiled. "It looks as though Sarah did escape after all."

Amy nodded. "The question is, does he know that?"

"Let's find out," Joe replied.

~

Peering from behind the bushes, Joe saw that the cabin looked deserted. He tried to see through the window, but it seemed to be even dirtier than before so he couldn't make out anything. He turned to Amy. "I'll go closer and try the door."

"Be careful," Amy said.

"Run if I yell out," Joe replied. Tiptoeing, he crept towards the building, not daring to make his presence heard by anyone close by. Not that he thought that there was anyone near, but it was better to be safe than sorry.

He reached the door without any trouble and took hold the handle. Before twisting it, he leaned forward and listened to see if there was anyone inside.

He could hear a faint noise. It was almost as though someone was squirming about. He could also hear someone muttering to themselves. Hoping that it was Will, he swung open the door.

It was Will, and he was all alone. The red haired boy smiled. "It's good to see you."

"Same here. I don't suppose you managed to get to the police?" Joe asked.

Will shook his head as Joe went behind his chair and went to work on the rope. "I tried, but they caught me before I could. Oh, have you heard about Sarah?"

Joe shook his head. "She stowed away on a rowboat a few hours ago, and we just saw the man who rowed it come back, but we didn't hear—"

"I heard everything." Will grinned. "She made it."

"Fantastic!" Amy exclaimed.

Joe whipped round and saw his sister standing by the door. "I told you to keep guard."

"I know, but I was worried—" Amy said.

"Okay, help me untie Will," Joe interrupted.

Amy went to work and, with Will helping as much as he could, it wasn't long before he was free. He stood up and stretched his arms. "That feels good."

"Let's not stand around talking." Joe hurried to the door and gazed out. No one could be seen. "Let's go." He raced off.

~

"So, does everyone know what they have to do?" Joe asked as he gazed up at the tree house.

"Yes, but I don't know why we can't just go from one place to another," Amy said. "The men can only search one spot at a time. Besides, the police will be here soon."

"Well, they should be, but we can't be sure. And, with the men looking for us, this seems to be the best place to hide." Joe looked up at the sky. "It will be getting dark soon, so let's get to work."

They split up, doing what needed to be done to get the tree house ready. While Will went to fill a bucket with sand, Amy gathered pine cones that were lying all over the ground and put them in a pile.

Meanwhile, Joe went and found some vines. Finding two long ones, he tied them between two trees that were located between the beach and the tree house. He hoped that the men wouldn't come before they were ready, but if they did, they might trip on them and that would give he and the others enough time to climb up to the tree house.

After telling Amy and Will about the vines so they wouldn't be tripped up, he climbed up the tree. When he reached the top, he tied the rope that they had to a branch and threw the rest down to the ground. Unfortunately, it didn't quite reach, so he had to tie it to a lower branch. This time it reached the ground.

When Will came back, he tied the bucket to the rope and waved to Joe who started hauling. It took a while as the bucket was heavy, but once it was at the top, he tipped the sand out on the planks and dropped the bucket back down.

This time, Amy filled it with pine cones. Once the bucket was full, Joe pulled it up. The cones were much lighter than the sand and, before long, they were also up on the platform.

"Is that enough?" Amy yelled.

"Let's get two more buckets," Joe replied. "Just in case. It's better to have more than less."

Amy, along with Will, disappeared into the bushes to collect more cones. After they had found some and they had been put in a pile in the tree house, Joe climbed down and joined the others.

They went to the campsite where Joe surveyed their belongings. "Anything that could be useful, we should bring to the tree house. Maybe even sleeping bags."

"That reminds me," Will said. "The pilot took my torch away from me."

"I wonder where my torch is." Joe turned to Amy. "Where did you last see it?"

"Well, we used it to explore the cave, then you let me use it at the lighthouse." Amy thought. "I remember lying down on that mattress. Oh, no."

"What?" Joe said.

"I think I took it out of my pocket when I lay down and I believe I left it there," Amy replied.

"Blow!" Joe said. "Someone will need to go and get it. We can't afford to not be without a light in case the police don't get here before nightfall and we have to hold off the men." He paused as he looked between Amy and Will. "It's my torch, so I suppose—"

"I'll get it," Will interrupted. "I know I haven't been inside the lighthouse before, but I can run faster than you two and that will come in handy if the men spot me."

"Is a torch really that necessary?" Amy said.

"Yes, it is." Joe turned to Will and handed him the rucksack which he had just emptied. "Take this in case you come across anything else in the lighthouse that we can use."

Will took it. "I won't be gone long." He turned and hurried away.

~

As Will came into sight of the lighthouse, he breathed a sigh of relief. There was no sign of the men and he hoped that it would remain like this.

Heading towards the rocks, he saw that the waves were splashing over them. Not every time, but more than half the time. He knew that high tide was only a few hours away so this was what he had expected. This was another reason why he had wanted to go instead of Joe. He felt he was a better swimmer and, in case he was swept off the rocks, he had a better chance of reaching the shore.

He had two options. Either run and hope for the best, or take it slow. Deciding that he would take a chance, he waited for a wave to crash onto the rocks and then, as soon as the water retreated, he ran.

As he arrived at the front of the lighthouse, he saw how much damage had been done. Joe had told him what had happened, but he hadn't realised how big the explosion had been.

He clambered over the pile of rubble and climbed up the steps. He passed the oil cans and, as he did so, a thought came into his head. Peering inside one of the cans, he saw it was almost full. He put the can inside the rucksack before continuing up the steps.

After reaching the room with the mattress, he searched around, hoping that he would spot the missing torch. He grinned as he saw it lying on the floor. Hurrying over, he picked it up and put it in his pocket.

There was no need to stay any longer, so he went back down the staircase. As he passed the cans, he decided they would need more than one, so he found two more and, taking one in each hand, headed to the rocks.

As he reached them, a big wave crashed over, showering him with spray. Without waiting for the next one, he raced over the rocks. He nearly slipped, but then he was off the rocks and on the grass. Glancing around, he couldn't see any sign of the men, so he set off at a brisk pace towards the tree house.

CHAPTER 23

RUNNING OUT OF TIME

It had taken Will a while to convince the others of his plan, but as soon as they had agreed, they went to work.

"Are you sure this is going to work?" Amy asked as she picked up one of the cans and spread the oil in a circle about six feet from the tree trunk.

"As long as it doesn't rain," Will replied.

The three went around the tree, pouring oil. Will's can wasn't as full as the others, so he finished first. Standing back, he made sure that the others were not pouring too close to the trunk. He didn't want to burn down the tree with them in it.

"I think that's enough," Will said after the others had gone around twice.

Amy dropped her can down. It hit a rock and fell on its side.

Will frowned. "Is that empty?"

"Ah, no," Amy replied as she reached down and righted it. "It has some oil left."

Will walked over and peered in the can. "We could drop it onto the men as they climb the tree."

Joe looked around. "We should see where the men are. Stay near the tree house in case I come back in a hurry." He hurried up the hill, glancing up at the sky as he did so. They had been pretty busy so he hadn't thought about the weather, but seeing the dark clouds that were heading towards him, he realised why it was so dark.

A storm was building. He didn't know what time it was, but with the sun behind the clouds, it made it much darker than it would normally be.

Reaching the top, he glanced around. There seemed to be movement by the church so he reached for the binoculars that hung around his neck and looked through them. Two men were talking. Turning to the inlet, he could see that the seaplane wasn't yet back. He had no idea where it had gone, but he was sure it would return.

He sat down, wanting to see what the men would do. They continued talking for a few minutes before they split up. He kept his gaze on the bald one whom he knew was the leader. The man walked to the beach and then to the woods before disappearing.

Joe waited for a few minutes before he thought he had better get back to the others. He stood up and started to go down the hill, pausing as he heard a noise. Stopping, he glanced to the side where the noise had come from. He waited to see what it was.

A moment later, the bushes parted to reveal Luke. Startled, Joe turned and ran down the hill.

Luke sprinted after the boy. "Stop! I want to talk!"

Joe heard the footsteps pound after him and he realised he needed to head for the vines and rope that he had placed between the trees. He changed direction and was nearly caught as the man reached out.

Joe swerved back and forth to evade capture as he raced through the bushes.

~

Sarah stared out at the raging water that seemed to grow more ferocious with every passing second. Dark clouds were gathering overhead and, while it hadn't yet started to rain, it looked very ominous.

Moving away from the railing of the police patrol boat, she headed towards the wheelhouse just as Quigley, along with Inspector Price, stepped out.

Sarah had only got to know the inspector two weeks earlier, but already she thought that the jovial, bald policeman was one of the nicest people that she had ever met.

"Are you going to land where we landed?" Sarah said.

The inspector glanced at the storm clouds. "It would be a tight fit in these conditions, so we'll try the inlet where the seaplane landed. If we can get in there, we'll also be a lot closer to the criminals."

"But will you have enough room if the plane is still there?" Sarah said.

"We should, according to the map, but only time will tell." The inspector looked at his watch. "We should be within sight of the island in five minutes, so excuse me while I make some last minute arrangements."

As the police inspector hurried away, Sarah turned to the old man. "Do you think the others are okay?"

Quigley put an arm around Sarah. "I'm sure they are. Why, I wouldn't be surprised if they already have the men all tied up."

~

As Joe rounded the corner he saw, with relief, the vine that he had tied between the two trees. Hoping that the man only had eyes for him, he leapt over it. He didn't glance back or slow down his stride, but as he heard a thud, he looked back. The man was lying flat on the ground.

Joe did a little leap for joy as he raced around the next bend and to the tree house. He yelled out to the others as he came in sight of them. "I just tripped up one of the men using the vines."

"What about the others?" Will asked.

"They weren't with him, but we'd better hurry and get up the tree," Joe replied.

Will kept look out as the other two climbed up. Once they were halfway up, he followed, grabbing the remaining can of oil as he did so. He heard a yell as he saw Luke run towards him.

As Joe and Amy had already reached the top by now, Will moved to one side and yelled out. "Throw the cones!"

Joe grabbed two, aimed, and let go.

Luke let out a yell as the cones made contact with his head. He shook his fist at them. "Just you wait!" He turned and hurried away.

Will resumed climbing and was soon at the platform. "Thanks for that. I was worried for a moment that he was going to reach up and grab me."

"He's probably gone to get the others," Amy said.

Will put the can that he had carried up into the corner and glanced around. "Let's make sure we're ready. Where's that pine cone, the one that we're going to use to light the oil with?"

"It should be somewhere in that pile," Joe said.

Will shuffled through the numerous pine cones until he found one that had a bit of cloth around it. "Good. Now, who has the matches?"

"I have them." Amy reached into her pocket and

frowned. "They're not here."

"Did you take them out?" Joe questioned.

Amy thought. "No." She searched in the other pocket and frowned. "There's a hole in this pocket. They must have fallen out."

Joe glanced around. "They could be everywhere."

The three of them quickly searched the tree house from top to bottom, but no matches could be seen.

Will peered down and caught sight of something. Taking the binoculars from Joe, he looked down. He grimaced as he saw the matches. "They're on the ground by the base of the tree."

"What?" Amy exclaimed. She looked down and saw that he was right. "Golly, what do we do now?"

"It would be risky to go and get them now," Joe said.

Will nodded. "I know, but someone has to. There's no way we can light the oil without the matches."

"Maybe we won't need to," Amy said. "The police should be here soon."

"But what if it turns out to be the difference between being captured or not?" Will looked towards the corner of the structure where the two paintings leaned against a branch. "We can't let the men get those paintings."

"If I hurry, I should be able to get back up in time," Joe said.

"I can go," Will offered.

Joe shook his head. "You went in the seaplane. It's time I did something. Yell out if you see any sign of the men."

Amy nodded as Joe started to climb down. "Will do." The seconds ticked by slowly as he got closer and closer to the bottom. Just before Joe reached the ground, she heard a low murmur of voices and realised it was the men. "The men are coming!"

Joe had stuffed the matches into his pocket when he heard Amy call out and he froze. Listening, he heard the footsteps. Glancing up at the tree house, he realised there was no way he would have time to climb up. There was only one thing to do. He yelled to the others. "Throw down the pine cone!"

The seconds ticked by and, as the men came into view, the pine cone fell towards the ground. After rushing over to it, Joe bent down and opened the box of matches. He was in such a hurry that the matches fell in every direction.

Marvin strode towards the boy. "Where are my paintings?"

With the matches falling all over the place, Joe grabbed one and lit it. Holding it below the rag, he managed to light it. With the men staring at him, he shoved the remaining matches into his pocket.

"Trying to scare us with a little fire, hey?" Luke sneered.

"It's not going to work, kid," Kenneth snapped.

As Joe backed towards the tree, he let go of the pine cone and flung it towards the oil. He watched it roll along the ground and hit the oily substance as Marvin walked towards him.

Nothing happened. Joe stared as the cone just sat there. As Marvin got closer, he realised that it was all over. Within moments, he'd be captured and the others would be forced to hand over the paintings.

All their hard work had come to nothing. And all because the pine cone, the most vital part of the plan, had not set fire to the oil.

CHAPTER 24

A RAGING FURNACE

Suddenly, there was a whoosh as the oil lit. Within a matter of seconds, it was a raging furnace.

With the searing heat warming his clothes, Joe turned and scrambled up the tree faster than he had ever done before.

It wasn't until he was halfway up that he dared look back down. He saw that the men had retreated to a safe distance away from the flames.

Joe resumed climbing and the others helped him up as he reached the platform. He collapsed onto the floor of the tree house as he recounted his close call. "I thought I was going to get captured. I really did."

Amy nodded. "Me too. It was too close for my liking."

Will patted Joe on the shoulder. "You did a good job. With any luck, the fire will keep burning until the police arrive." He looked down once more at the fire and grinned. But, within moments, his grin had turned to a frown. "Hey, did any of you put oil close to the tree?"

Joe sat up and joined Amy as the two of them glanced down and stared at the spot that Will was looking at. A spot of fire was burning halfway between the trunk and the circle.

Joe frowned. "That's weird."

"Maybe some of the oil dripped," Amy said. "Anyway, does it really matter?"

"As long as it doesn't come too close to…" Will paused as the fire reached the trunk and started going up it.

"How could oil get on the tree?" Joe questioned.

Will shrugged his shoulders. "I don't know." He turned towards the can of oil that he had brought up earlier. "I wonder."

"Wonder what?" Amy said.

Will took hold of the can and peered inside it. It seemed as though it was almost empty. Tipping it upside down, he saw a hole. "Oh no! The oil was leaking out." Will looked back down the tree and saw that the fire was gradually moving upwards.

As it did so, the others connected the dots. Joe pointed to the can. "So that's why the fire is on the tree trunk."

"The hole probably occurred when it hit that rock," Amy said, disappointed. "It's all my fault."

"No, I should have realised it was getting lighter," Will replied. "I just hope that not a lot dripped out."

"Is there anything we can do?" Amy asked.

Will shook his head. "No. We just have to hope that the fire dies out soon."

As smoke started to drift upwards, Joe sighed. "It looks as though we have gone from one lot of danger to another, except this one is much worse."

Will nodded. "And whatever happens is out of our hands."

~

With a pair of binoculars glued to his eyes, Inspector Price watched as a seaplane landed in the inlet. The wind blew it towards the beach and, within moments, it had beached itself on the sand.

Standing by the railing, Sarah looked back at the patrol boat that was following them. "How many men do you think we have?"

Quigley shrugged. "Don't know, but it will be enough." He turned as he saw the seaplane. "It looks like they haven't left…" He stopped speaking as shots rang across the inlet.

As bullets began hitting the side of the craft, the inspector turned and yelled to the captain. "Turn it around on the double!"

Quigley and Sarah dropped to the floor straight away and stayed there as the vessel swung around. But the inspector didn't move. Peering through the binoculars, he tried to see where the shots were coming from.

He saw a man by the seaplane. He got out his pistol and aimed it towards him. He pulled the trigger twice and watched in satisfaction as the man retreated.

"Did you hit him?" Quigley asked.

"No, I only scared him," the inspector replied. "But it's too dangerous to land men here in case the other criminals are lying in wait." He looked at Quigley. "What's the next possible landing spot?"

Quigley frowned. "Well, this was the main one. You could always take your chance on the rocks, but in these conditions—"

"No, we can't take any chances," the inspector said. "I want these men brought to justice and I want it done before the sun goes down."

"What about the place where the others and I landed?" Sarah suggested.

Quigley nodded. "That's the only other one. It will be a tight fit with the dinghies, but better than taking a chance on the rocks."

The inspector yelled out to a police officer. "Take her around the island."

~

Just as Joe was wondering if the fire would go out or not, thunder broke overhead and rain poured down. He had forgotten about the mass of dark clouds that he had spotted half an hour or so ago. The three of them huddled underneath the branches as the rain pelted the area.

"This will put the fire out," Will said.

"Good," Amy said. "I was getting worried that the fire was gaining ground."

Joe looked down and saw smoke drifting up as the fire was smothered. He couldn't see any sign of the men. He turned to the others. "If the rain continues like this, the men might not climb up."

As the minutes passed, the rain continued to pour down. Lightning flashed nearby and thunder crackled overhead as the storm intensified.

"We don't normally get storms like this in summer," Will said.

"It's a good thing we're getting this one," Joe replied, speaking louder so the others could hear him over the noise of the pouring rain.

Several minutes passed before the rain started to ease. Thunder still rumbled in the distance, but a minute later, the rain had stopped.

Peering down, Joe saw the men emerge from beneath a tree and head for the tree trunk. As he watched, Luke and Kenneth began climbing up.

"When shall we use the pine cones?" Amy said.

"Now!" Joe grabbed a pine cone and hurled it. It sailed past Luke, missing him by a foot. "Blow!" He took another cone and threw it down. This time, it hit Luke on the head. He yelled out, but continued climbing.

A torrent of pine cones rained down upon the men as they climbed up. As soon as Luke reached a branch, he hid underneath it.

Joe turned to the others. "We have to hold the men off as long as possible, so don't throw another cone until they move."

Amy and Will nodded. The men didn't move for a minute and then, after glancing up, resumed climbing. The children threw down more pine cones.

"Let's use the sand," Joe said as he noticed that they were getting low on pine cones. After grabbing a handful, he let it go directly above the men. Being wet, it stuck together as it fell, and it had almost the same effect as the pine cones.

"Yes!" Joe cried out as it hit Luke on the forehead.

For the next five minutes, sand was thrown down and the men yelled out as most found their target. But, before they knew it, the sand was all gone. "We'll have to use up the rest of the pine cones," Will said.

The pile got smaller and smaller as the two men ducked back and forth amongst the branches as the children used up the rest of the pine cones.

As Joe reached to grab another one, he realised that Will had just picked up the very last one. He and Amy watched as Will peered over and dropped it.

It was right on target. Luke hid underneath another branch, as did Kenneth.

Will glanced around the empty tree house. Only a rucksack, torch, and the two paintings remained.

"What do we do now?" Amy asked.

Will looked down and saw that the men were still not moving. "We hope that the men stay where they are."

"I'm sure the police must be on their way," Joe said. "We just need a bit more time." As he heard Marvin yell out, he glanced down and saw with annoyance that Luke and Kenneth had emerged from their hiding places and resumed climbing. He turned to Will who was looking through the binoculars to see if he could see any sign of the police. "Can you see anything?"

Will shook his head. "No."

CHAPTER 25

A LEAP OF FAITH

Reaching the inlet, the two patrol boats came to a stop. The inspector shouted orders to his men as a dinghy was lowered from each craft into the heaving water.

Climbing into the lead dinghy, the inspector yelled out to Sarah and Quigley. "You two come with me."

Sarah climbed down into the craft as the wind whipped at her blonde hair. For once, she was glad that she didn't have long hair like her sister.

As Quigley joined her in the dinghy, two officers took the oars and started rowing towards the inlet. Followed by the other craft, they headed towards the frothing water, where rocks could be seen above the surface.

With Quigley helping with the directions, and Sarah yelling out every now and then, they were able to pass the rocks and reach the beach.

As the officer threw the oars on the sand, the inspector waved at the patrol boats to show that they were okay before heading up the side of the cliff.

~

Will looked down at the men who were now not far away. "We don't have any pine cones left, so we need to get away from here. If I tie a rope to that nearby tree, we could climb down it and escape."

"But how are you going to get across to it?" Amy asked looking at the gap that was between the branches.

"I've climbed many trees before, so I'll be fine," Will said. "As for that gap, I'll jump."

"Just be careful," Amy said.

"I will." Will tied one end of the rope around a thick branch before tying the other around his waist. Climbing out onto a branch, he edged along it.

Amy looked down at the men. "If only we had something else to throw down."

Joe suddenly thought of something. "I've got an idea." He knelt down on the platform and lowered himself onto the first of the wooden footholds.

Looking down, he saw that the men had another five or so to go before they reached him. Knowing that he had to be fast, he climbed down another two footholds. Then, with Luke closing in, he grabbed an upper branch with his hands and, gripping tightly, stomped down onto the foothold.

It moved slightly. He tried again. It moved yet again.

"Hey! Stop!" Luke yelled.

Joe glanced down and saw the man hasten his pace. He realised he only had one chance. One last chance to slow down the men. One last chance to stop them from getting the paintings. It was all up to him.

Taking a deep breath, he gripped the upper branch as hard as he could, raised his feet off the foothold, and pushed them down onto the wood with all the force that he could muster.

Nothing happened.

For a moment, Joe thought that it was all over. Then, suddenly, the wood gave way. Breaking into two pieces, it tumbled down, nearly hitting Luke in the face. Joe grimly smiled, but he couldn't relax or shout out for joy yet. The battle may have been won, but the war was far from over.

He swung his legs to and fro before they landed on another branch. Standing on it, he pulled himself up onto the next foothold. He considered doing what he had done to the other one, but he realised it would be hard, if not impossible to do. There was no overhanging branch which meant that he would have nowhere to place his hands.

If the foothold fell, he would go down as well. To fall at this height would mean a serious injury, so that was out of the question. Anyway, as he looked down at the man who had now reached the place where the foothold used to be, he could see that he had delayed him.

It was possible to climb up using the branches and not the foothold, which he would now have to do, but at least it had slowed the men down.

Climbing up onto the platform, he was just in time to see Amy wrap her end of the rope tightly around a thick branch. She looked towards him. "Did you slow them down?"

"Yes, but not for long." Joe peered across to the other tree and saw that Will was safely across. He waved and Will waved back.

Joe turned to Amy. "You'd better go next."

"Shall I take the paintings or will you carry them?" Amy asked.

"I'll carry the rucksack." Joe watched on as Amy took hold of the rope and, with both hands clutching it tightly, stepped out onto a nearby branch.

It was slow going for Amy, and as Joe looked down at the men and saw them trying to climb up, he knew that time was running out. But he didn't say anything.

He didn't want his sister to rush and fall.

He watched as she reached the spot where she had to jump off the branch and land on the branch connected to the other tree. This was the trickiest bit and one that would require the biggest amount of concentration on her part.

Holding his breath, he waited for Amy to jump. It seemed like forever as he watched her steady herself. Then she jumped.

As she clutched the other branch and held on, Joe sighed with relief. Tearing his eyes away from her, he looked down at the men.

They were making progress, much faster than he would have liked. After going to the rucksack, he put the two paintings inside and put it on.

He waited until Amy had reached Will before he grabbed the rope. He hadn't wanted to hold onto it until she had finished, but maybe he should have.

Glancing down, he saw that Luke was almost at the platform. He realised that as soon as he went across, the man would follow him. He needed to find a solution and fast. An idea came into his head. One that was so wild that it might just work.

Joe yelled to Will. "Tie the rope to a higher branch."

"What? Why?" Will asked.

"Just do it!" Joe yelled.

Will obeyed, and as he climbed up to a higher branch with the rope, Joe looked down at the edge of the platform as a hand became visible. He needed to get moving.

"What are you doing?" Amy shouted.

Joe didn't answer as he untied his end of the rope as Will gave a wave and a nod to indicate that the rope was now tied.

Joe moved to the edge of the platform and stood

where there was nothing blocking his way. If he crashed into a tree going fast, it would not be a pretty sight.

Looking back to see where the men were, he saw Luke clamber up onto the platform. He had to go now. He turned around and told himself to step off, but he couldn't.

He muttered to himself as he tried to urge himself to step off. But he couldn't. This was worse than all of his previous hair-raising escapades, such as being dragged along the water in Smugglers Cove and climbing up the cliff near Bracknesh Castle.

"Give me the paintings, boy," Luke called out. "I won't hurt you. I just want the paintings."

"No!" Joe shouted, glancing back. "Never."

"Why, you..." Luke snarled as he reached out his hand to grab the rucksack.

Joe pulled the rope tight, closed his eyes, and stepped off.

~

The inspector peered through the binoculars as he looked towards the church. He was able to see two people beside the building. "Okay, men, let's move in before it starts to rain again." He looked towards Sarah and Quigley and then at an officer. "Stay with those two here. I don't want them in harm's way." He ran down the hill.

Sarah turned to Quigley. "I want to see if the others are safe."

"I'm sure they will be," Quigley said. "As soon as all the men are caught—"

"I don't want to wait that long," Sarah interrupted. "If you don't want to go, I'll go by myself."

As she walked off, the police officer yelled out. "Hey, you're supposed to stay here until the inspector comes back."

Sarah paused for a moment. "I'm going to find my brother and sister." She then raced off towards the woods.

~

As soon as Joe heard the wind whip past his face, he opened his eyes. Everything seemed to go in slow motion as he sailed closer and closer to the ground.

He could hear Amy and Will shout out, but couldn't understand what they were saying. Gripping tightly to the rope, he hung on for dear life.

The ground seemed to rush towards him and he grimaced, expecting to smash into it. But, luckily that didn't happen. As Joe swung back and forth, with each swing getting smaller than before, he looked up at the others and waved.

They waved back and he grinned with relief. Stepping off had been the most scary thing that he had ever experienced, and he had lived to tell the tale.

As the rope slowed down, he jumped onto the ground. Touching the dirt with his hands, he was glad to be on solid ground once more.

~

High in the trees, the others watched as Joe hurried to the tree that they were sitting in. Suddenly, he tripped, falling flat on his face.

"Oh no!" Amy exclaimed.

Will watched in horror as Marvin appeared from behind a tree and grabbed the paintings from the rucksack. "He must have been waiting for Joe and tripped him up."

"And we can't do anything," Amy muttered.

The two of them could only stand still and watch on as the man, with a painting in each hand, took off running.

Amy saw Joe stagger to his feet. She didn't think that he would race after the man who already had a good distance on him, and she was right.

Joe yelled up to them, "Sorry. There was nothing I could do."

Will turned to Amy. "I guess that's it then."

Amy sighed. "I guess you can't win all the time."

CHAPTER 26

GOODBYE ADVENTURE ISLAND!

Sarah was halfway down the hill when she spotted someone coming towards her. Hiding behind a tree, she saw it was Marvin. He was clutching a painting in each hand.

Sarah didn't know what was going on, but she knew that she couldn't let him escape. She saw that if he continued going in the same direction, he would pass very close to the tree that she was hiding behind.

An idea crept into her head. Hunting around, she picked up a long, thick stick and knelt down behind the tree.

Listening carefully, she heard Marvin approach. The seconds seemed like minutes as she waited for the right moment to put out her stick. She couldn't put it out too soon in case the man saw it, but she couldn't put it out too late either.

With both hands on the stick, she suddenly thrust it out. Two seconds later, his feet hit the stick and Marvin stumbled before falling to the ground.

As he scrambled to his feet and glared at her, she realised she hadn't given a thought to what to do next after she had tripped him up.

Marvin glared at her. "Just wait till I catch you."

He stomped towards her angrily and she stumbled backwards, frightened.

Turning, she tripped over a rock and fell down. Before she could get to her feet, Marvin was standing over her.

Just as Marvin went to grab Sarah, a voice yelled out. "Hold it right there!"

Seething with anger, Marvin reluctantly raised his hands.

Sarah grinned as she caught sight of a police officer and Quigley hurrying towards her.

The police officer had his pistol out and it was aimed at Marvin. Taking out a pair of handcuffs, he snapped them onto his wrists. "Get going up the hill."

Marvin grunted as he turned and walked up the hill, but not before he glared at Sarah one last time. But before he could say anything, the officer pushed him forward.

Sarah turned to Quigley and hugged him tight. "Thanks."

Quigley comforted her. "It's okay now." He glanced down at the ground at the two paintings. "What are those?"

Sarah picked up the tubes and looked at the nametags. "Vincent van Gough."

Quigley chuckled. "Well, well, no wonder he was angry. They'll be worth a couple of hundred pounds." As he heard voices, he looked down the hill and smiled as he saw Will, Joe, and Amy along with a police officer.

Sarah followed his gaze and yelled out in delight as she raced towards them. She could tell that they were disappointed. "What's wrong?"

"Marvin got away with the paintings," Joe said. "We tried our hardest, but—"

"You mean the paintings by Vincent van Gough?" Sarah interrupted.

Joe frowned. "Yes, but how did you know?"

Sarah smiled as she looked towards Quigley. He was holding the two paintings in his hands.

The others followed her gaze and smiled in delight. "How did you do it?" Amy cried out.

"I saw him coming and I tripped him up," Sarah replied, her green eyes shining.

Amy hugged her little sister. "I was worried about you."

"And I was worried about you too," Sarah said. "Did you hear that Inspector Price is here?"

"Yes," Will said. "We were at the tree house when we saw the pilot rush past. Before we could stop him, several police officers, along with the inspector, appeared. We told them where the other men had disappeared to and they rushed off, but not before the inspector told us where you were."

"Let's go to the top of the hill and see if we can see them," Joe suggested. As the others nodded, he turned and headed up the hill, the others following close behind.

~

Darkness had fallen by the time the patrol boat pulled up alongside the pier. The criminals were led down the gangplank and five police officers, who had been waiting patiently on the pier, took them away.

As the children walked down the gangplank a few moments later, they heard a shout. Looking along the pier, they saw their parents rushing towards them. Yelling out, the four children ran and hugged them.

Mr Mitchell smiled at the inspector as he joined

them a few moments later. "Thanks for bringing them home."

Inspector Price grinned. "It's the least I could do after Sarah told me about the art thieves. You might not know it, but we've been after that particular bunch of criminals for two years."

"What about Nancy?" Joe asked. "Was she really part of the gang?"

"From what you told me earlier, and from the quick chat I had with the criminals, I would say that she is Susan Thomas, someone we've had our eyes on for some time," Inspector Price replied.

"Will you try to catch her?" Will questioned.

"We'll do our best, but I don't have high hopes," the inspector replied. "Anyway, we've caught the rest of the criminals, so there's no chance of the operation starting up again. So, good job."

"It was more luck than anything," Joe admitted. "After all, if no one had been on Windswept Island, we would have camped there and then we wouldn't have seen the men."

"But it was still a brave effort on your part." The inspector looked at Will. "Your escape to France might not have turned out the way you expected it to, but the good thing is that it enabled us to catch the men flying the seaplane as well." The inspector turned to Sarah. "Hiding in that rowboat must have been hair-raising at times, and from what I've heard about the bicycle chase, you had quite an adventure."

Inspector Price glanced at Amy and Joe. "You two also did a good job. If you hadn't delayed the men by stealing the paintings, then they probably would have made their escape long before I arrived at the island. So, good job all of you."

He looked up as Quigley joined them. "And if it

wasn't for you, we wouldn't have had such an easy time making landfall at the island."

Quigley smiled. "I just had to help. I wouldn't want nothing to happen to these nice kids. They're a good bunch."

"It's a shame about the boat, though," Will said.

"Especially after all the time we spent painting it," Amy added.

"It was a dear little boat," Sarah piped up. "I'll miss it."

Inspector Price smiled. "Don't worry. I just remembered something that should raise your spirits."

"What?" Joe asked eagerly.

"There was a reward offered for anyone who could give us information about the art thieves, and since you helped us catch them, you are entitled to it," the inspector replied.

"How much?" Will asked.

"I don't know exactly, but it'll certainly cover the cost of a new sailboat." Inspector Price looked at his watch. "It's getting late. I'd better go and take care of the criminals. I'll be in touch with you soon."

"Thanks once again for bringing them back safely," Mr Spencer said.

The inspector waved his hand dismissively. "It was my pleasure. After all, it's not every day four children help you catch a gang of criminals that you've been after for more than two years." He turned and walked away.

Joe looked at his parents. "You'll never believe the adventures we've had."

"You should have seen the tree house," Amy said. "We had to—"

"Why don't you tell us in the car?" Mrs Mitchell suggested as she looked at her watch. "It's getting quite late."

"My, so it is," Mr Spencer exclaimed. "We'd better be going too."

As the parents walked to where they had parked their cars, Will turned to the others. "Even though the men took me hostage, I still enjoyed solving the mystery of Rocky Island."

"It should be called Adventure Island, just as Quigley called it," Amy said. "After all, everyone who goes there seems to have an adventure."

Joe laughed. "The mystery of Adventure Island. I like the sound of it. So, how about we meet up at Darby's tomorrow for an ice cream?"

"What for? To discuss the next mystery?" Will teased.

"No, but that isn't such a bad idea." Joe grinned. "After all, we still have two weeks before we go back to school, so let's make the most of it. Oh, and last one to reach the cars has to buy the ice creams!" Joe raced off down the pier.

"Hey! Wait!" Amy shouted. She ran after Joe, determined not to be beaten.

Made in the USA
Middletown, DE
30 October 2018